A PEACHY CASE

SWEET PEACH BAKERY #4

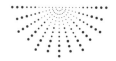

WENDY MEADOWS

MAJESTIC OWL
PUBLISHING LLC

*M*omma Peach liked Seattle and she sure loved the majestic beauty of the Pacific Northwest. Seattle was an interesting city with lots to do and see, with lots and lots of rain following you everywhere like a lonely friend seeking comfort. The landscape surrounding the city was absolutely breathtaking—the tall, lush trees, fertile forests, diamond-clear lakes, beautiful valleys and rugged coastline all combined into one gorgeous jewel. The land was sure different from Georgia, yet the places seemed connected, like it was all one sweet voice from heaven.

"I sure liked walking around Seattle with you, Mr. Sam," Momma Peach said, looking out of the backseat window into a heavy rain. The taxi was carrying them to the port where the North Queen was resting at the dock, and the driver maneuvered his way away from the fancy hotel and onto a rainy highway filled with wet cars.

Sam glanced over at Momma Peach. Momma Peach was wearing a bright pink rain jacket over her blue and white dress. Her hair was covered with the usual pink cloth that somehow seemed perfect. "Your face is shining," he said in a relaxed voice.

"I am happy, Mr. Sam," Momma Peach replied. She looked at Sam. Sam was dressed like a cowboy ready to tame a few wild horses. "I sure am happy you decided to come along on the cruise. And I like your new cowboy hat, Mr. Sam. It makes you look tough."

Sam grinned. He lifted his right hand and felt the hat and then glanced down at the rugged brown jacket he had tossed on over a pair of old blue jeans. "Old habits, Momma Peach...old habits." Sam walked his eyes out into the rain. "That restaurant we ate at last night sure had some good food, didn't it?"

Momma Peach patted her belly. "I don't have any complaints," she chuckled. "I especially ain't complaining about the chocolate mousse."

Sam's grin widened. "I noticed."

Momma Peach chuckled again and nudged Sam with her elbow. "Silly."

Sam smiled and glanced back over his shoulder. The cab

Michelle and Able were riding in appeared behind them on the wet highway. "Michelle sure seems to like Able, doesn't she?"

"My baby girl is in love," Momma Peach confirmed. She reached into her purse and pulled out a piece of peppermint. "I think I hear wedding bells."

"Really?" Sam asked, shocked. He watched Momma Peach place the peppermint into her mouth. "Michelle and Able just met."

"I know that, baby," Momma Peach smiled. "But sometimes a heartfelt prayer is answered quicker than lightning can flash down from the sky."

"Married...wow...I just can't imagine Michelle married." Sam leaned back in his seat. "She's...I mean, last night she got into a fight with that cabbie who tried to overcharge us."

Momma Peach stopped smiling. "I saw her tangle with that tattoo-covered bear," she said and shook her head. "What choice did she have? That ugly bear tried to shove her up against the cab."

Sam made a pained face. "That was the guy's first and last mistake. I doubt he'll try to cheat anyone again." Their cab driver glanced in the rearview mirror at Sam but didn't say a word. Perhaps their driver had heard about his friend being beaten to a pulp by some kung fu-fighting cop.

"I think so, too," Momma Peach agreed. She looked over her shoulder and spotted Michelle's cab. "Michelle wants peace, Mr. Sam, but she won't ever back down from a fight." Momma Peach attempted to cheer up her heart. "But her new boyfriend sure didn't let his woman take on that ugly old bear alone, now did he?"

Sam thought back to the fight and how Able had jumped on the back of Michelle's opponent. He laughed. "Able sure tried to hold on, but that bucking bear was too much for him."

"Bless his heart," Momma Peach said and felt a smile touch her lips again. "Able may be the clumsiest man alive, but he sure ain't no coward. No sir and no ma'am. He might end up getting himself shoved in a garbage can someday, but he'll do so fighting with all his might."

Sam agreed. "Able will protect Michelle, that's for sure...and Michelle will always protect him, too. I guess you're right, Momma Peach. Those two are meant for each other...two heartbeats finding each other like lost boats on a lonely sea."

Momma Peach looked into Sam's face and saw sadness. "Mr. Sam is thinking of his wife."

"Hard not to, at times, Momma Peach," Sam confessed.

Momma Peach patted Sam's arm. "I know, baby," she assured Sam. "But listen to me, okay?"

"Okay."

"I won this cruise and I want all of my friends to have a grand old time. So," Momma Peach patted Sam's arm again, "I don't want you feeling sad. We're gonna get on a big old ship that's going to take us up there to Alaska. We'll be far away from all our troubles, Mr. Sam. Of course," Momma Peach shook her head, "I sure don't know what kind of troubles we might return to. I must have been crazy to leave Old Joe alone with Mandy and Rosa. Oh, give me strength."

Sam winced. "Yeah, I'm not sure what we're going to return to, either, Momma Peach. Old Joe is...well, let's just say I carry my wallet in my front pocket when he's around."

Momma Peach laughed. "Don't I know it, baby. Old Joe is an old dog set in his ways. I guess he'll always be an old shyster. But at least he's changing...some."

Sam laughed and patted his back pocket. "Just making sure...yup, I still have my wallet."

"Oh, you," Momma Peach said and nudged Sam with her elbow again.

"I reckon men like Old Joe just need time," Sam told Momma Peach. "I'm sure Mandy and Rosa won't put up with any scheme he might come up with, either."

Momma Peach nodded her head. "My girls can handle

Old Joe. I can just picture it...if he gives them any lip they'll simply lock him in the cellar and stand on top of that trap door until Old Joe promises to behave himself." She and Sam chuckled mightily at the image in their minds.

The cab driver continued toward the dock without saying a word and decided to take a shortcut so he could charge an honest fare. When he arrived at the rainy dock, he quickly unloaded the luggage in the trunk and accepted the fare skittishly from Sam before driving away into the rain at top speed. "What's with him?" Sam asked Momma Peach.

Momma Peach opened a bright pink umbrella and cast her eyes up at the biggest ship she had ever seen in her life. The North Queen was docked quietly in the port with the stormy waters of the bay beyond. The ship was rocking back and forth a tiny bit in the troubled waters but standing tall, with lonely blue and white colors wrapped around it. A strange feeling gripped Momma Peach's stomach. The sight of the cruise ship terrified her for some unnamable reason. "Oh my," she whispered, staring through the hard rain at the massive ship with its boarding ramp extending down to the dock a little ways further down from where they stood. The cruise ship loomed back at her, its portholes looking out like mysterious eyes that were, she thought, filled with fear.

Having exited their own taxi, Michelle and Able walked

up to Momma Peach. "That's a really big ship," Able said in a worried voice, holding a gray umbrella over Michelle's head with his left hand and a brown suitcase in his right hand. "I hope I don't get seasick."

Sam winced. He could all too easily imagine Able getting seasick. The poor guy looked bad enough wearing his dorky red and green striped rain jacket. Of course, Able thought the jacket was cool and Michelle didn't have the heart to say otherwise. Michelle, on the other hand, looked very stylish in her black leather jacket zipped tightly against the rain over a dark gray dress. Sam supposed opposites did attract. "Maybe you should go see the ship's doctor once we're underway?"

"Good idea," Able agreed. He looked at the cruise ship with worried eyes.

Michelle squeezed Able's hand to reassure him. She was so happy to be on vacation with the people she loved. Being in Seattle with Able had been very romantic. The shopping was fun. The food was delicious. The landscape was gorgeous. Now she was about to board a fancy cruise ship and sail north to Alaska. But one glance into Momma Peach's eyes sent all of her wonderful feelings running away into a dark corner. "Momma Peach?" she asked.

Momma Peach heard Michelle say her name, but she didn't reply. She was staring at the cruise ship in a hypnotic state. "Oh my," she whispered again, scared.

Michelle stared at Momma Peach. "Momma Peach?" she asked again.

This time Momma Peach managed to tear her eyes away from the cruise ship and look at Michelle. "Yes, baby?"

"Are you okay?"

Momma Peach looked into Michelle's beautiful face. Just last night she had seen Michelle standing outside of a cozy restaurant with Able in the rain, laughing and giggling and so happy. Her baby was having a splendid time—well-deserved and well-earned. How could she spoil the fun by putting into words what her heart was telling her? "I'm fine, Michelle," Momma Peach promised and forced a smile to her face. "I guess we...better get on board before that big old ship sails out to sea without us. Mr. Sam, are you ready?"

"Ready as ever," Sam smiled. "Able?"

Able gulped. "Ready...as ever. Honey?" he asked Michelle.

Michelle had not stopped staring into Momma Peach's face. Something was wrong. "No, I'm not ready," she said. "Momma Peach, what is it? I can read your eyes. Something is the matter."

Momma Peach looked back at the cruise ship. Beyond the cruise ship was the rough, open sea filled with hard, choppy waves. Momma Peach sighed. "Baby, a bad feeling came over me just as soon as I laid eyes on that ship."

"A bad feeling?" Able asked, alarmed.

Sam didn't say anything. Instead, he stared at the cruise ship with curious eyes. "Yes, a bad feeling," Momma Peach confirmed. "The sight of that big old ship is scaring me something awful."

Michelle looked up at the ship again. She felt a strange feeling sweep over her. Before she could say a word, Sam spoke up. "Yeah, I'm getting a bad feeling in my gut, too." Sam wasn't lying to make Momma Peach feel better, either. He was speaking the truth: the sight of the cruise ship had made his gut knot up just then.

"Do we...get on board, then?" Able asked.

Able's question was answered by a loud fire alarm erupting on board. Momma Peach darted her eyes around the ship and spotted black smoke pouring out of an upper deck. Employees of the cruise line scurried to the boarding ramp and began rushing passengers off the ship and then hurried to safety themselves. Soon there was quite a crowd huddled on the dock. "What's going on?" Sam asked a middle-aged man in a white cruise line uniform who was striding past them.

"Major kitchen fire," the man told Sam and shook his head. "We couldn't get it under control...the fire is spreading. You better stand back. The fire department will need room when they arrive."

"So...no cruise?" Able asked.

"Not today," the man said firmly, and hurried off.

Michelle looked at Momma Peach. "I guess the cruise is off," she sighed. Despite the fearful feeling of panic that she had felt in her gut just moments before, Michelle was heartbroken.

Momma Peach felt relief and sadness engulf her heart. Surely it was better to be on land and watch the cruise ship burn than to be at sea when it happened, when they would surely have been shoved into lifeboats and simply praying for the best. But still, the disappointment in her Michelle's eyes broke her heart. "Maybe not," Momma Peach said and looked at Sam. "Maybe...we can rent a car and drive to Alaska?"

Sam folded his arms together. "Now there's a good idea. Able, Michelle? What do you think?"

Able stared at the black smoke rising up from the ship. The ship seemed cursed in his eyes. "Yeah, driving to Alaska seems a lot better than sailing."

Michelle considered Momma Peach's suggestion. She imagined being on the open road with Able, sitting together in the backseat, holding hands, stopping at log cabin restaurants, sleeping in rugged bed and breakfasts, or camping under the stars and roasting marshmallows. "I think driving to Alaska will be fun," she smiled. "It's obvious our ship isn't going out to sea anytime soon."

Momma Peach looked at the cruise ship. The ship seemed to look at her with hurt eyes now. Momma Peach knew, deep down in her heart, that she would see the cruise ship again. "Well, no sense in standing around in the rain. We better call a cab to take us to a car rental place and—oof!" A man wearing a dark gray trench coat jolted into Momma Peach and almost knocked her over. "Excuse you!" Momma Peach growled as she caught her balance. The man rushed off and vanished into the crowd of panicked employees and passengers. Michelle began to give chase, but Momma Peach grabbed her arm. "Let him go, baby."

Michelle watched the man vanish and shook her head. "Some people," she said and looked at Momma Peach. "Are you okay?"

"I'm fine, honey." Momma Peach looked at Able. "Able, why don't you go call us a cab."

"I'll go with him," Sam said, not trusting the younger man not to get lost in the commotion and walked off with Able.

Momma Peach deliberately turned her back to the cruise ship. "We'll put this morning's events behind us and have a wonderful trip. You'll see. We'll get up there to Alaska and tussle with some grizzly bears and tickle the bellies of some salmon."

Michelle smiled at her words, but her eyes watched Able and Sam weaving away through the crowd in the rain. Then she turned and saw that the black smoke was growing thicker and thicker. In the distance, the sound of sirens began whining. "Come on, Momma Peach, let's get out of this rain. There isn't any sense standing here."

"You ain't too disappointed about the cruise, are you?" Momma Peach begged as they turned to walk away.

Michelle shook her head. She wrapped her arm around Momma Peach and smiled. "Momma Peach, as long as we're together, that's all that matters to me. And to be honest, I was kinda worried Able might get seasick and spend the entire cruise in the bathroom. At least now," Michelle added in a positive tone, "he can't get seasick."

Momma Peach smiled. "No," she agreed. "Let's just hope he doesn't get car sick, baby," she said with a chuckle and walked off with Michelle. She looked over her shoulder at the cruise ship and knew that she was going to see the North Queen again somewhere, but for now, she was happy to put it behind her.

"Wow, so the kitchen was deliberately set on fire?" Able

asked, sitting in the back seat of a gray minivan with Michelle.

Sam focused on the road before him. Tall, beautiful pine trees lined both sides of the road. Beyond the trees stood the towering peaks of the Alaskan wilderness; untamed, wild, rugged and free. Sam imagined what the land looked like covered with snow. Summer was winding down and fall was quickly approaching. Before long, the land would be blanketed with fresh, white snow. "Seems that way," he said.

Momma Peach stared out of the window at the beautiful landscape from the front seat. They were about two hours away from where they planned to stay at the Snowy River Lodge. Not that she was in any rush to get to the lodge. The drive up into Alaska from Seattle had been relaxing and peaceful so far. But Momma Peach couldn't seem to get her mind off the North Queen. Her heart felt unsettled. "Yes," she told Able, "some scoundrel set the kitchen on fire, they're saying in the newspaper. We saw it in a copy of the local paper at the last gas station, while you boys were in the rest room."

"Why arson?" Able asked.

"Exactly my question," Michelle answered Able. Her detective's mind was awake and she was focused on the fire despite the beautiful landscape around them. "An employee or employees had to be involved."

13

Sam eased down his window a bit to let in some fresh, clean air. He drew in a deep breath. "Will you smell that air," he said in a voice that told everyone he wasn't in the mood to continue discussing the misfortune that had struck the cruise ship. "The air is cooler up this way than it was down in Juneau."

"We're north of Anchorage," Able pointed out. He looked out of the window next to him and soaked in the untamed landscape. "I wonder if there are any grizzly bears around?" he asked.

Momma Peach felt a smile touch her lips. Leave it up to Able to make a worried woman smile. She unfolded her arms and brushed a few wrinkles out of her blue and white dress. "Honey, if there are bears, Momma Peach will run them off for you."

Able nervously swallowed. He wasn't interested in tangling with a grizzly bear. "The lodge we're staying at...it's pretty remote, huh?"

"Very remote," Sam confirmed happily. "We're going to be two hours from any town."

Michelle reached over and touched Able's hand. "It'll be cozy," she promised. "When the man back in Juneau told me about the lodge, I knew it would be a great place to visit."

"And it was one cop to another, so we know we can trust him," Sam reminded Michelle. He glanced at her in the rearview mirror. "I'm glad you ran into that retired cop. I didn't say anything, but I was hoping to get in some good fishing. Now it looks like I'm going to be able to."

"The lodge...isn't in any tourist brochures, though," Able worried. He had spent their stop in Juneau anxiously scanning the racks of brochures for a different kind of hotel—the kind where the nearest wildlife was safely enclosed in a zoo.

"That's what makes the lodge a great place," Sam assured Able. "Word of mouth is the only way anyone can find out about the Snowy River Lodge. Way up here in the wilderness, folks don't need fancy brochures. All they need is a good, honest reputation."

"That's right," Momma Peach agreed. She reached into her purse and pulled out a peppermint, hoping to distract Able from any further worries. "Anyone want a peppermint? I have plenty."

"I'll take a peppermint," Able spoke up. Momma Peach handed him one. "Thank you, Momma Peach."

"Michelle?" Momma Peach asked Michelle.

"Sure," Michelle smiled.

Momma Peach handed her the peppermint and then looked into her eyes. "I think it might be awful wise for me and you and all of us to forget all about that old cruise ship."

Michelle hesitated. "I don't like coincidences," Michelle told Momma Peach.

"Do you really believe the fire set on the cruise ship was because of us?" Sam asked Michelle. He hated to dive back into the topic but couldn't keep himself from asking. The truth of the matter was that he didn't like coincidences either—and it seemed awfully coincidental that Momma Peach won four cruise ship tickets and then the trip was canceled due to a deliberately set kitchen fire.

"I can't say for sure," Michelle answered honestly. "Maybe not. But I did some checking back in Juneau and found out that the North Queen, the cruise ship we were going out to sea on, has had some serious issues."

"Like what?" Able asked.

"Well, for instance," Michelle explained, "the North Queen has been docked for electrical problems, plumbing problems, engine room problems, the works. All just in the last year, even though it's a relatively new ship. Also..." Michelle hesitated to mention her next bit of information but knew that Momma Peach deserved to hear the truth. "There was a murder that took place on the North Queen last year."

"A murder?" Momma Peach asked. A cold pit formed in her stomach. There was silence in the van as the trees rushed by them, and the landscape suddenly looked much colder than it had before.

"A businessman by the name of Callahan Minson was found drowned in an exercise pool in a private gym below decks. The North Queen has a public gym open to everyone, and another private gym for passengers who pay extra for the privilege." Michelle paused, gathered her thoughts, and continued. "Minson was on board because he was showing interest in buying out Blue Wave, the company that owns the North Queen and its cruise line."

"Sad," Sam said and shook his head. "Murder is a horrible crime."

Momma Peach sat silent. In her mind, she saw a dead body floating in a swimming pool. The North Queen was a cursed ship after all. It was a relief to know she had not been imagining things. "Anything else, baby?" she finally asked.

"The North Queen underwent repairs and renovations last year and was approved for voyage a few months ago. Our trip up the coast to Alaska would have been the North Queen's first voyage since the murder of Callahan Minson," Michelle explained. She looked at Able and saw worry in his eyes. "Perhaps it was a blessing that a fire was set. No one was hurt, but no one had to travel on a ship with such bad memories, either."

"Seems to me someone wanted the ship grounded again," Momma Peach stated. "Perhaps whoever set the fire wasn't counting on a fire investigator figuring out the arson so soon...perhaps they wanted it to look like just another mechanical problem or electrical fire. Then again, maybe whoever set the fire did it in a way that could only point to arson?"

Sam glanced over at her. "Momma Peach, we're way up here in Alaska and that ship is way down there in Seattle. I think we should all put the fire behind us and focus on enjoying our vacation."

"Sam has a good point," Able said. He looked at Michelle with hopeful eyes, but then his brow wrinkled as a thought occurred to him. "I'm not an expert on cruise lines, but from the facts you've gathered, it could also be that the Blue Wave cruise line company might be sabotaging its own ship in order to collect insurance money."

"What about the murder?" Michelle asked Able. She felt a strangely warm and calm feeling embrace her. Having Able in her corner somehow made her feel like everything—no matter the problem—was going to be okay.

"Could it be this Mr. Minson wasn't who he was pretending to be?" Able suggested, intrigued. "Perhaps Blue Wave had a motive to get rid of him. Mr. Minson might have been a mole from their competition, not really a good-faith investor. Or he could have been an undercover insurance agent. Who knows?" Able mused for a moment, then shook his head as if to clear his thoughts and patted Michelle's soft hand. "Honey, I agree with Sam. Let's focus on enjoying our vacation. Focusing on a problem you can never solve isn't healthy."

Michelle stared into Able's caring eyes. She smiled. "Of course," she agreed. Able was right. It was exciting to think it through, but why focus on a case that she could never solve? What was done was done and the cruise ship was hundreds of miles away. She leaned toward him. "You know, it's going to be a clear night. I was hoping that we could start a campfire tonight and sit outside under the stars."

"I like that idea," Able told Michelle and softly squeezed her hand. "Sam, before we arrive at the lodge, do you think we can stop at a local store? We need marshmallows."

Sam smiled. "You bet," he promised. "I think we're coming up on the last store before we get to the lodge." Sam pointed to his right. Momma Peach saw a small dirt parking lot with a single gas pump. A small log cabin was set back from the pump, pushed up against the trees. A carved wooden sign identifying it as Wilderness Supplies and Gas hung over the front window like a welcome beacon. Sam slowed down, eased into the parking lot and pulled up in front of the gas pump. "Might as well top off the tank," he said. "And," he added, "if anyone needs to make a bathroom break, now's the time. We're still a good two hours away from the lodge."

Michelle grabbed her leather jacket and slung it on over her light pink dress. Able grabbed his dorky rain jacket and popped it on. Momma Peach decided to embrace the cool air and skip her jacket. "I will get us some snacks," she told Sam.

Sam nodded his head and hopped out of the driver's seat. He stretched his arms and drew in a deep breath of air and looked around. The land was calling out to him. It wasn't that he didn't like Georgia, his recently adopted home—but sometimes, deep down, he felt that he needed more. His eyes drifted over to the log cabin store. For a few seconds, he imagined owning the store. The feeling swelled his heart.

Momma Peach walked around the front of the minivan and saw Sam staring at the log cabin store. She saw the expression in his eyes. Her heart broke. There stood Sam, wearing his cowboy hat, a dark blue button-down shirt tucked into a pair of old jeans, and brown cowboy boots. The man just looked like wilderness personified. "Mr. Sam, is there anything special you want me to get you?"

"Huh...oh," Sam said and shook his head. "Uh, a bottle of water and maybe a pack of trail mix, if they have some?"

Momma Peach walked over to Sam and tucked her arm

into the crook of his elbow. She looked up into his eyes. "You ain't happy in our little Georgia town, are you?"

Sam stared down into Momma Peach's eyes. "Momma Peach," he answered honestly, "I'm not a town person. I don't like being around a lot of folk. I guess I'm just an old hermit. But I'm also getting old and need more than just solitude. Sure, I could live out here in this wilderness and be free as a bird," Sam shook his head, "and die without anyone noticing or anyone who...cares about me. As much as I don't like being around a lot of folks, some folks sure matter." Sam leaned down and kissed Momma Peach on her cheek. Momma Peach nearly began crying. "Why don't you go inside and see if this place has some of your peppermints? You don't want to run out."

"No, I sure don't need to run out of my peppermints," Momma Peach agreed and wiped at a single tear. She looked over her shoulder and saw Michelle and Able smiling at them. "Okay you two, the show is over. Inside."

Michelle walked over to Momma Peach and took her hand. "Old Sam isn't leaving us," she promised. As Michelle began to speak again, a red truck raced past the log cabin store at breakneck speed, its engine roaring unnaturally in the quiet. The truck sped down the road and vanished around a curve.

Able shook his head. "Probably some very bored local kids," he said and looked at Sam. "How much gas you want?"

"Oh, we're close to half a tank...better pay twenty," Sam told Able.

Momma Peach gazed around at the rugged landscape. Alaska sure was beautiful. She pictured herself owning the little store, selling peach bread to snowed-in winter folk, shoveling snow, building snowmen, drinking hot cocoa, sitting beside a warm fire on a snowy night, quilting a blanket. The feeling was cozy and welcoming. But Momma Peach also knew she was a Georgia woman and Georgia was where she belonged. Who else would fuss over the terrible food down at the local diner? But then again, her meddlesome Aunt Rachel wouldn't be able to find her. That thought put a smile on Momma Peach's face. She began humming as she walked toward the log cabin. Michelle and Able followed.

Momma Peach walked up to the heavy wooden door. She pulled the door open and stepped into a room that smelled of cherry tobacco smoke and pine wood shavings. The old hardwood floor creaked under her feet, and her eyes were drawn to the knotty pine walls crammed with mounted prize fish and antlers, and framed photos of men with rifles standing over dead game. A wood stove stood in the middle of the room casting out enough heat to keep a gray metal coffee pot warm on top of it. "Hello, folks," an old voice greeted Momma Peach.

"Hello," Momma Peach replied and walked up to the wooden front counter. She spotted an old man sitting on a stool. The old man was reading a newspaper and didn't seem to have a care in the world. "Nice place you have here."

The old man put down his newspaper next to an antique cash register and looked up at Momma Peach through a pair of thin reading glasses. He couldn't count the times folks had complimented his store. "You want to buy it?" he asked.

"Really? It's for sale?" Able asked, looking around. He spotted a wooden shelf displaying snacks. "Hey, candy bars," he said in a happy voice.

The old man smiled. "Nah, this old place isn't for sale," he teased, his eyes twinkling good-naturedly at Momma Peach. "The wife and me still have some good years left."

"You bet," Momma Peach beamed. She studied the old man. She found his thin gray hair, intelligent face, and green flannel shirt very soothing. "We're going up—"

"Up to my brother's lodge," the old man finished for Momma Peach. "Yeah, Mitchel phoned me and said he had some folks coming up his way. I guess that red truck that sped past here a minute ago is heading up to the lodge, too."

Michelle watched Able pick out a candy bar and a bag of marshmallows and smiled. Able looked so happy. "I'll take a candy bar, too, honey," she told Able.

"And trail mix. Don't forget Mr. Sam's trail mix," Momma Peach called out over her shoulder. "Do you have any peppermints?"

"No, afraid I don't," the old man told Momma Peach with a sad expression. "Wait..." the old man rummaged under the counter and pulled out a red and white peppermint tin can and winked at Momma Peach. "Why, I guess I do." He opened the tin can and looked at Momma Peach. "Take all you want."

Momma Peach grinned. The old man nearly had her. "Silly," she said and took a few peppermints. "Now tell me, Mr. Wilderness Store, how does a person survive way out here in the wilderness?"

The old man tapped Momma Peach's purse. "Open your pocketbook and I'll tell you."

Momma Peach opened her pocketbook. The old man leaned forward and poured the entire tin can of peppermints into her pocketbook. "We survive by taking care of one another," he said and winked at Momma Peach. "Way out here, folks are more than neighbors. Folks become family. In my younger years, I worked as a lawyer in Portland, Oregon. I began losing my heart to the ways of the world and knew I needed change. Came to Alaska in 1971 and been here ever since."

Momma Peach felt an immediate love for the old man. "Well, I know all about family, honey, and I can tell that you're one good fella that is welcome in my heart and my family, any time. See my girl Michelle over there?" She indicated Michelle, who was standing next to Able at the candy display, a fond smile on her pretty face. "She's a police detective." Mama Peach swelled with pride to see how impressed the old man looked. She continued, "You can probably guess we're not blood related. But she is my family, just as sure as the Lord's stars shine above."

The old man nodded wisely and turned a gentle smile back to Mama Peach. "Well, then. I think you're going to love the bright stars you can see here in Alaska."

Outside, Sam stood beside the gas pump and waited for the old man inside to turn it on. While he waited, he spotted a flash of color in the distance, where the curve of the road disappeared around the bend. When he squinted, he could see the tail lights of the red truck they had just seen. It had backed down the road just enough to spot him and the rest of the parking lot. The truck idled there for a minute, and then raced off again.

CHAPTER TWO

*M*omma Peach stepped out of the minivan and felt her mouth drop open. "Oh my," Momma Peach said.

Sam walked over to Momma Peach and put his arm on her shoulder. "Will you look at that view," he said in a soft voice.

"I am in love," Momma Peach told Sam as her eyes soaked in the view of a large, clear blue lake at the foot of a majestic mountain. She saw beauty mixed with wonder, mystery, danger, romance and a hint of something extra, she thought. Mama Peach knew that extra spice in all this beauty could only be the freedom that comes when you live in a world not controlled by money and traffic.

A cozy two-story lodge made from massive timbers and logs spoke of the strength of the trees that had been harvested for its construction. Snowy River Lodge stood on a small hill, overlooking the lake and the small, sparkling river that twisted through the valley below. The lodge appeared rugged, yet very warm and welcoming, Mama Peach thought. It was homey, even. A large stone chimney stood on the north wall of the lodge. Smoke was coming from the chimney. The wood smoke smelled of an early winter whispering promises of heavy snow. Momma Peach looked up at the chimney smoke and then back down at the lake. "I wonder if that lake freezes over in the winter?"

"It's possible," Sam replied and squeezed Momma Peach's shoulder. "I'll grab Able and get our luggage. Why don't you take Michelle inside and get us checked in?"

Momma Peach smiled. "I can do that."

Momma Peach turned and saw Able with his arm around Michelle. They were standing near the back of the minivan staring down at the lake. The late afternoon sun was reflected in sparkling diamonds across the lake. "So beautiful," Michelle whispered.

"Like you," Able said and then blushed.

Momma Peach stared at Michelle. The happiness resonating from her was precious. "Michelle, I'm going to go inside and get us checked in. You coming?"

"Oh," Michelle said quietly and smiled into Able's eyes. "I guess that's my cue."

Able gently kissed Michelle. "See you later."

Michelle blushed and hurried off with Momma Peach, but not without checking the gravel parking area first. She had romance on the brain, but she could never shake her cop's habit of checking her surroundings for threats. The red truck they had seen speeding past the log cabin store was parked at the far end of the parking lot. Michelle didn't think much of the truck, except to hope that the guests who had arrived in the red truck would be quiet so that she could enjoy her time with her friends, and especially her time with Able. She was hundreds of miles away from all of her troubles. The nearest town was two hours away. What kind of trouble could possibly be waiting here, other than perhaps a cheeky raccoon scavenging for leftovers after dark? "I'm so glad we decided to drive to Alaska," she told Momma Peach. "The cruise would have been nice, but...crowded. This is so much better."

Momma Peach squeezed Michelle's hand and smiled. "I know, baby," she said and tossed a quick glance at the red truck and then walked up a stone pathway lined with old logs. The pathway took them to a large front porch holding comfortable rocking chairs and a table with a checkerboard. Momma Peach climbed up the seven wooden steps and paused. The sight of the front porch called out to her. She grinned and then hurried over to an old rocking chair sitting off by itself and sat down. "Oh, I am definitely in love."

Michelle giggled. She loved to see Momma Peach's short little legs swing beneath her as she rocked in the tall chair. "It's very peaceful," she admitted and drew in a deep breath of clean, fresh air. "You can smell the trees, the ground, the lake, the sky...the freedom!" she exclaimed.

"Freedom is right, baby," Momma Peach agreed, looking around with satisfaction. "I love my bakery and I love Georgia. But sometimes it's good to get away from all we know and be in a place that is untouched by man's greedy paws. I know this is the way the good Lord intended for folks to live. Not crammed in next to each other in an overcrowded city or sitting in traffic trying to get to a worrisome job just to give other folks your money." Momma Peach began rocking back and forth again in the rocking chair. Oh, how she wanted a slice of her peach pie and a glass of cold milk. Yes, sir and yes ma'am. "That beautiful lake out there is freer than we'll ever be. The cold waters of that lake must have some mighty sweet dreams. But we humans...we just don't seem to get it, baby. We're too busy trying to hurt and kill each other with cold hearts."

Michelle glanced back toward the minivan and saw Able helping Sam unload the luggage. She remembered it hadn't been so long ago that Able had lived a sad city life just like the one Mama Peach described. Michelle imagined Able living back in Philadelphia, crammed up in a small apartment, working for the company that had treated him sourly and unfairly for too long. Her heart broke. She nearly began to cry. "Momma Peach, is it wrong to want to stay in Alaska forever?"

"No baby, it's not," Momma Peach confessed. "Sometimes the heart hungers to be free from the world we call home." Momma Peach stopped rocking and slowly stood up. She stretched her back and walked over to a heavy wooden front door. "Let's go inside and get checked in, honey."

Michelle followed Momma Peach through the front door and they stepped into the large, rustic lobby that smelled of pine wood and cherry tobacco smoke—the same cherry tobacco smell she had smelled back at the log cabin store. "Wow."

"Wow is right," Momma Peach whispered. Her eyes soaked in a large green and brown hand-braided rug in the middle of the lobby. Eight dark brown armchairs, arranged in pairs, were placed around the fireplace in comfortable positions. Each pair of chairs had a coffee table between them that held books. A large stained-glass window stood on the north wall; the gentle colors filtering through it seemed to be humming a sweet song. "My," Momma Peach said, delighted to see the cheery fire in the large stone fireplace and a gray coffee pot hanging over the fire.

Michelle smiled. She pointed at a hand-carved bookshelf holding four potted plants. "Look at all those books! I can imagine sitting in front of that fireplace on a snowy night, a cup of coffee in hand, reading a cozy mystery."

An old man that was an exact copy of the old man back at the log cabin store stepped through a door behind the front counter. He waved a hand at Momma Peach and Michelle. "Welcome! I'm Mitchel Stewart. I was wondering when you folks were going to arrive."

"Well, I'll be," Momma Peach said and hurried over to the front counter. She rubbed her chin and studied Mitchel's face. Then she grinned. "Why, that old coot back at the store got me again."

Mitchel stared at Momma Peach with confused eyes and then understood. "Oh, I see my brother didn't mention that we were twins."

Michelle walked up to the front counter. She looked at the red flannel shirt Mitchel was wearing and then glanced up at the narrow pair of reading glasses on his nose. Mitchel's appearance set a warm peace in her heart. "My name is Michelle Chan. This is Caroline Johnson. But we all call her Momma Peach."

"Momma Peach is my name," Momma Peach beamed.

"Momma Peach it'll be then," Mitchel promised. "Your men are still gathering the luggage. I spotted them from my living room window."

"Oh," Momma Peach blushed, "Old Sam ain't my

gentleman. Mr. Sam is a sweet man and I love him, but I have my husband waiting for me up in heaven."

"I see," Mitchel replied in a respectful voice. "My wife of fifty-two years passed away two years ago. I guess it won't be long before I join her. Sometimes these long winters can be mighty tough on a seventy-four-year-old man."

"Why do you stay, then?" Michelle asked. "Why not relocate to an area that is easier to live in?"

"Well, Detective Chan," Mitchel replied and cast a loving smile at Michelle, "my wife and I built this lodge with our own hands. Oh, we had help, of course, but it was our sweat and determination that turned a run-down cabin into what you see today. A man just can't get up and walk away from a place he has carved his life into."

Michelle stared at Mitchel. No one had ever explained a home to her before in those terms. "Yes, sir," she said.

Momma Peach smiled, catching something Michelle had not remarked upon. "You know Michelle is a cop, huh?"

"My brother gave me a call. He told me about this pretty woman," Mitchel winked at Michelle. "Now, let me see if I have your reservations right." Mitchel turned and fiddled with a stack of papers. "Ah, here we are." He turned back to Momma Peach and Michelle. "You reserved four rooms and you'll be staying with me for two weeks?"

"My idea," Michelle confessed. "I even called my boss and asked to extend my vacation time. I...haven't taken a vacation in a few years and had a lot of time saved up. I used a few of my vacation days recently in Nevada, but still had plenty of days left. I...wanted to spend time with my new...uh...friend." Michelle blushed. Mitchel smiled. "I sound silly, don't I?"

"You sound like a woman who is in love to me," Mitchel promised Michelle. "Oh, to be young again," he said and tipped Momma Peach a wink. Momma Peach winked right back. "Well, except for you folks, we only have one more guest staying with us. A quiet fella. I don't think we'll be seeing much of him. The fish might, though."

Momma Peach looked over her shoulder and spotted a wooden staircase leading up to the second floor. The lodge had a total of eight guest rooms, and behind the front lobby was a dining room and kitchen, and a small gym and laundry room. The second floor held the guest rooms as well as a reading room and game room. The first floor was also home to a small apartment that Mitchel lived in. Momma Peach wasn't certain where this quiet fellow was. "Is your guest upstairs?" she asked.

"Nah," Mitchel said. "Too pretty of a day. Saw him head out about twenty minutes ago with a fishing rod in his hand. He probably took the old trail down to the lake. And speaking of trails," Mitchel's voice became firm, "I have the trails marked. Do not go off my trails. I can't be responsible for folk getting lost." Mitchel shook his head. "I usually get some folk that like to come up here during the snow months. I have ski trails and hunting trails and fishing trails and hiking trails marked everywhere. But every so often, some darn nincompoop strays off the trails and gets himself lost. One fella...well let's just say I didn't find his body until spring." Mitchel shook his head. "Please, ladies, stay on the marked trails."

"We will, sir," Momma Peach promised. "I don't feel like getting lost and becoming a Momma Peach bear treat, no sir, and no ma'am. Oh, give me strength!"

Mitchel nodded his head. "This is the Alaskan wilderness. As you both know, the nearest town is two hours away. We're on our own up here. I'm on my own up here. My helper, Mrs. Dunsberry, had to leave last year because her son and his wife needed help with their new baby." Mitchel sighed. "Didn't really see no sense on hiring anyone after her. Truth is, business has been slow lately. Even in the winter months, tourism just trickles in and out. Been that way for the last few years now, ever since that new ski lodge was built. I used to have to turn folks away...now I'm blessed if I get any guests at all."

Momma Peach reached over the counter and patted Mitchel's arm. "So that's why your cop friend back in Juneau told us about your lodge."

"I have some close friends who advertise for me," Mitchel nodded his head. "I never could bring myself to advertise

35

in brochures or travel magazines…stuff like that seemed…unclean, to me. Word of mouth was enough. At least it sure used to be. That new ski lodge sure puts a damper on business. Folks just seem to want new and fancy things, I guess."

Michelle heard the front door open. Able trudged in with two armfuls of luggage. Sam followed behind him. They walked up to the front counter and set the luggage down onto the floor. "Getting colder outside," Sam said. "I'm used to the desert heat."

"Winter will come early this year. I can smell the snow in the air already," Mitchel told Sam.

Able explored the front lobby, peering around through his glasses. "Nice," he said in a strangely peaceful voice; a voice that told Michelle he could stay at the lodge for the rest of his life. The idea occurred to her, too.

Before Michelle could reply to Able, a tall man built like a rugged grizzly bear stepped through the front door and closed it with a hard hand. He glared at the front desk with cold eyes and then tromped upstairs holding a fishing pole in his right hand. The man looked very familiar to Michelle. "Hey, isn't that the man who bumped into you?" she asked Momma Peach in a shocked voice.

Momma Peach thought back to the rainy port in Seattle. She closed her eyes and saw a cruel-eyed man bump into her and walk away without saying a word. That man had been wearing a black rain jacket and a black Army skull cap. The man had also sported a thick black beard. The man that walked upstairs had a clean-shaven face. "I...can't say for sure," Momma Peach confessed. She opened her eyes and looked at Michelle. "Baby, the man who bumped into me had a beard, remember?"

"Yeah, I remember," Michelle said, staring up at the stairs. "Maybe...I'm just tired. It's been a long ride." Michelle forced a smile to her lips. "What are the chances, anyway?" she asked. "I guess I'm being a bit paranoid. After all, we only got a glance at the man who bumped into you. I only saw his face for a split second."

Sam looked over at the staircase. A knot formed in his stomach. The man who drove the red truck was not sitting well with him, not at all. When he looked back at Momma Peach, he saw that her eyes were uneasy, too. "I say we all go to our rooms, take a long hot shower, get some fresh clothes on, and meet for supper." Sam turned to Mitchel. "What's on the menu tonight?"

Mitchel paused, startled. He didn't like the look on Michelle's face. Michelle was a cop. Cops—good cops— had solid instincts. "Uh, hamburger steak, baked potatoes, green beans, salad...and for dessert, peach pie."

"Oh, give me strength, the man said peach pie," Momma Peach said and forced her worry away. What were the chances the man who bumped into her in Seattle was now staying at the same remote lodge she and her friends had found? "Mr. Mitchel, baby, you ain't tasted peach pie until you tasted one of my peach pies. Let me get freshened up and then I'll come back down and bake you the best pie you've ever eaten."

Marc Stravinsky walked into the dim lodge room, tossed down the fishing pole he was holding into a corner, and sat down in a green armchair under a window covered with a thick green curtain. Anger was pulsing under his cold skin. Menace was seeping from his ice-blue eyes. "I have to be very careful," he whispered in a low tone. "I will have to kill them off one by one."

Marc reached into the shapeless gray jacket he was wearing and pulled out an ugly gun. He stared at the gun and then stuffed it back into his jacket pocket, stood up, and walked over to a nightstand sitting beside a king-sized bed covered with a heavy red and white quilt. He focused on the brown phone sitting on the nightstand. "It's time," he said and snatched the phone up.

Mitchel picked up from the front desk immediately. "How can I help you, sir?"

"I need to place an outside call."

"Long distance calls will be deducted from your room deposit," Mitchel explained.

"That's fine."

"You'll have to come down to the front desk and place your call," Mitchel informed Marc. "The room phones only connect to the front desk."

"I see," Marc said and squeezed his left hand into a tight fist. "I'll be down in a minute."

Marc slammed the phone down and threw his eyes toward the window. He had loose ends to tie up, and he would begin with Momma Peach. "It was stupid to slip those matches into that woman's pocket," Marc growled, condemning his knee-jerk reaction back at the rainy port in Seattle, and then left his room. Once he killed Momma Peach, he would return to Seattle and eliminate the president of the Blue Wave cruise line company, collect his dough, and escape to Europe. As Marc walked down the hallway, he knew he was passing the room that was Momma Peach's, and he knew it wouldn't be her room for long.

Momma Peach was inside her room, standing at the bedroom window and staring down at the beautiful lake. Her mind was at ease and her heart felt rested. "Oh, how lovely," she hummed sweetly, allowing her eyes to soak in the beauty of the crystal clear lake. She saw herself taking a stroll around the lake, holding wild flowers in her hand, taking deep breaths of crisp, cold air as she walked under a sky pregnant with snow...oh, how peaceful was the thought. "I could surely live up here, even with the bears."

A knock on the bedroom door brought Momma Peach back to reality. "Who is it?" Momma Peach called out.

"Sam."

"Come in, Mr. Sam. The door is unlocked," Momma Peach called out. She turned from the window and watched Sam open the bedroom door and walk into the room. Sam appeared relaxed and a little sleepy. "Everything okay with you, Mr. Sam?"

Sam closed the bedroom door and pointed at a soft pink armchair. "Can I sit down?"

"Make yourself at home, baby."

Sam plopped down in the sitting chair and rubbed his face. "Momma Peach?"

"Yes?" Momma Peach asked.

"I spent a few minutes talking to Mitchel and...well, even though he's not ready to sell this lodge yet, someday he will be. I...well, I signed up to be the first person in line." Sam looked up at Momma Peach. "Mitchel said it'll be a few more years before he's ready to sell, and that's okay. But when the time comes, I really want to buy this lodge. I've only been here two hours and I'm already in love."

Momma Peach smiled. "I figured as much, sugar. I can

also see there's more to this little announcement. Talk to me, baby."

Sam leaned back in the sitting chair. "When the time comes to buy this lodge, I want you to help me run it. You, Michelle and Able. I'll live here full time and you three can come and spend the spring months with me...or live here full time if you want. But I don't think you want to leave your home in Georgia."

"No, baby, I love my Georgia," Momma Peach told Sam in a gentle voice. "But when the time comes for Mr. Mitchel to sell, I will help you run your lodge."

"Our lodge," Sam corrected Momma Peach. "Momma Peach, I don't intend on dying for a good many years, but I went ahead and altered my will. I'm leaving all I have to you. I know you'll do what's right concerning Michelle. I want you to make sure that girl is happy. I'm very fond of her."

"I know you love Michelle as much as I do, Sam."

"I'm starting to think of her like she's my own daughter," Sam confessed. He smiled at Momma Peach. "I know what I'm saying is premature, Momma Peach. Mitchel let me know that he's got a few good years left in him, too. But in time, I really want to buy this lodge. Maybe...I'm being a bit childish, huh?"

"How so?" Momma Peach asked.

41

"Oh, because I lost my town and now I'm searching for a substitute. I hope I'm not being foolish or hasty." Sam rubbed his face again. "I like remote locations, Momma Peach. This lodge...there's something special about this place. I can see myself living here, snowed in, drinking coffee next to that great fireplace downstairs."

Momma Peach walked over to Sam and rubbed his right shoulder. "You are homesick for what you once had."

Sam looked up into Momma Peach's loving eyes. "I guess I am. I admit that the desert took a lot of adapting to, but once I settled in, I became part of the desert. I can see myself becoming part of this land, Momma Peach. But...not alone. If buying this lodge means losing you and Michelle, then I won't."

Momma Peach felt a sweet tear touch her eye. "Mr. Sam, I will come to your...our lodge and help you shovel snow. I will want to come to our lodge during the snowy months and have hot chocolate."

"Really?" Sam asked in a hopeful voice.

Momma Peach nodded her head. "Yes, sir and yes ma'am," Momma Peach spoke softly. She smiled. "Mr. Sam, I ain't getting any younger myself. Now, I have my bakery to run and pies to bake, but I also have a big enough heart to let the lodge become a second home to me because home is where family is. And Mr. Sam, I know you are my family and family makes a place home."

Sam stared up into Momma Peach's face and saw a glowing love that soothed his tired heart. "Yes, Momma Peach, family is what makes a place home."

Momma Peach's smile widened. "Also, I ain't seen a whole lot of snow in my life," she teased Sam and tossed him a wink. "Oh, give me strength, I am going to become an icicle up here with the bears. Move over and let me get next to the fire, have mercy!"

Sam laughed. He stood up from the chair and hugged Momma Peach and then kissed her cheek. "You're something special, lady," he said and left with a smile, and Momma Peach was alone in her room once again.

Momma Peach touched her cheek and smiled to herself and then decided to begin unpacking. She walked over to the king-sized bed and admired the white and pink quilt her suitcase was sitting on top of. "Mrs. Mitchel had good taste, rest her heart and soul," she said and opened her suitcase. The first item Momma Peach pulled out of the suitcase was her rain jacket. She walked over to a closet door, opened it, and took out an empty coat hanger for her rain jacket. As she did, a box of matches fell out of the left pocket of the rain jacket and dropped down onto the floor.

"Now, what is this?" Momma Peach asked. She quickly hung up her rain jacket, bent down, and picked up the box of matches. "Lake View Motel." She read aloud the name, which was scribbled on the front of the matchbox in red and blue lettering. "Now wait a second, I don't remember staying at no Lake View Motel and I surely didn't pick up any matches at the fancy hotel in Seattle." Momma Peach stared at the box of matches and tried to place them but failed. "Now, where did you come from?" she asked. And then, like lightning flashing out of a thunder cloud, she knew. "That buzzard who bumped into me at the rainy port...he could have slipped these matches into my pocket...and these here matches could have been the very matches that were used to start that awful kitchen fire on that doomed ship. That means..." Momma Peach stopped talking. She turned and looked at the room door and felt her gut begin whispering warning messages to her.

Momma Peach quickly steadied her mind and forced her eyes away from the door and began searching the room. She needed a place to hide the matches. "If a buzzard broke into my room and started to search for this here box of matches, where would he not look?" Momma Peach asked herself. She thought for a few seconds and then rushed into the bathroom and found an unopened roll of toilet paper sitting on the brown wooden counter next to the sink. She pulled the paper wrapper out of the top of the roll, stuffed the matches down into the toilet paper tube, replaced the paper, and put it back down next to the toilet. "That should do for now," she said, and set her mind on going downstairs to speak with Mr. Mitchel.

As Momma Peach stepped out into the hall and eased her

room door closed, she felt an icy chill, and turned to see the male guest walking down the hallway toward her. She steeled herself.

He approached her with a cold face and looked deep into her eyes. "You going to do some fishing, lady?" he asked.

"I like to fish," she said, preparing to slap the man standing before her upside the head with her purse if need be. The man's eyes were soulless and cruel. Momma Peach didn't like looking into eyes like that. Eyes like that gave her the willies.

"Be careful in these woods...accidents can happen," Marc warned Momma Peach in a menacing undertone, leaning in closer.

Before Momma Peach could say a word, Michelle stepped out of her room and spotted Momma Peach. She ran up to her. "Step away from her," she yelled at Marc.

"Or what?" Marc asked Michelle. "What are you going to do?"

Michelle stepped in front of Momma Peach. She looked into Marc's dead fish eyes. "I'm Detective Michelle Chan and I'm warning you to step away from this woman right now."

Marc gritted his teeth. "I don't like cops."

"And I don't like your bad breath," Michelle snapped at Marc. "Step back, now."

Marc looked past Michelle and locked eyes with Momma Peach. "Accidents, lady," he warned her and began to walk away.

Michelle grabbed his arm. "Hey, you can't threaten her." She used the force of her grip to spin him backward on his heels.

"Bad move," he growled and threw a punch at Michelle. Michelle ducked out of the way, maneuvered behind Marc, kicked him in the back, and sent him flying down the hallway. Marc landed hard on his front side. He began reaching for his gun but stopped when Sam and Able rushed out of their rooms. Too many witnesses. He climbed to his feet and brushed off his shirt. "Your girlfriend has a temper, pal. You better control her or else," he warned Able and stormed off to his room.

Able ran to Michelle. "What was that all about?" he asked.

Michelle looked at Momma Peach. "Are you okay?"

Momma Peach reached out and hugged Michelle. "You are always saving me from the bad guys," she said. "Now listen, baby, that buzzard is the same man who bumped into me in Seattle. I am sure of it now."

"I am, too," Michelle told Momma Peach. "I only got a quick glance at him in Seattle, but I got a good look at him just now. He's the same man."

Sam rubbed his hands through his hair. "But why?" he asked, confused.

"I will explain later," Momma Peach told Sam. "Babies, we have to be real careful of that man. He came here to make sure we never leave...or at least make sure I never leave." Momma Peach pointed at Michelle's room. "Michelle, bring your belongings to my room, please? I ain't sleeping alone. Mr. Sam, you double up with Able. And no matter what, we stay together."

"Why not just leave?" Able asked worriedly. He didn't like the sight of Marc. The man worried his insides.

"Because I can't let that snake loose to hurt other people, baby," Momma Peach told Able. "Whoever that man is, he's deadly and he's out to cause harm. If we run, he'll either follow us or just go hurt someone else."

Sam drew in a deep breath. "In other words," he told Able, "it's our duty. If we turn away from our duty, our conscience will suffer the consequences for the rest of our lives." Sam looked at Momma Peach. "Are you absolutely certain that's the same man, Momma Peach?"

"Yes, Mr. Sam," Momma Peach promised. Momma Peach grabbed Michelle's hand. "Come on, all of you, downstairs. We need to talk to Mr. Mitchel."

Momma Peach hurried downstairs and found Mitchel at the front desk sipping coffee from a brown mug. Before they could tell him what happened, however, they could see that his face was already very worried. "Mr. Mitchel?" Momma Peach asked. "What's wrong?"

Mitchel leaned over the desk and lowered his voice. "I've never listened in on a guest phone call in all of my years, but...when that man called out of here," he nodded at the ceiling to indicate the guest, "I knew to listen...and I did not like what I heard on the call." Mitchel set down the brown mug in his hand. "I'm wondering, what do I do? Do I call Sheriff Sarrings? Even if I did, it'll take that man over three hours to get here. He drives as slow as dripping syrup. And what would he do anyway? Scold me for listening in on a guest phone call and then bungle the investigation? Not to mention that horrible man just might kill us before the sheriff could even get here."

Michelle grabbed Momma Peach's hand. Momma Peach looked into Michelle's worried eyes. "I know, baby," Momma Peach said and looked up at the ceiling.

Upstairs, Marc oiled his gun with a dirty rag, listening closely for any sign of movement in the hallway. Revenge coiled in his gut like a viper ready to strike. He was devising a plan to kill everyone at the lodge, but he did not know that he would be dead before morning arrived.

CHAPTER THREE

*M*itchel leaned his elbow on the front counter, leaned down, and rubbed his forehead. "We have a killer upstairs," he whispered in a low voice. "His name is Marc. I heard him tell another man," Mitchel raised his eyes and looked up at Momma Peach, "that he was going to kill you first and then work his way down."

Michelle knelt down and retrieved her gun from the ankle holster wrapped around her right ankle. "Not on my watch," she told Mitchel.

"Maybe not," Mitchel agreed, grateful to have a cop present. "The man he spoke to ordered Marc to stand down and wait for him to arrive. It seems like this other man doesn't want violence at all." Mitchel shook his head. "He talked like a smooth business man...but his voice was corrupt. I could tell."

"The second man is coming here?" Michelle asked.

Mitchel nodded his head. "Mr. Heath Penlin called me a few minutes after our snake slithered back upstairs. I...made the reservation. What else could I do? I didn't want to take a chance and stir up unneeded trouble. Mr. Penlin seems to be in control of whatever is happening."

"You did what was right, Mitchel," Momma Peach promised him. "I would have done the same thing. You lured the cobra out of its nest. The only question is...if this cobra doesn't want me dead, then what does it want?"

Mitchel shrugged his shoulders. "The conversation lasted maybe a full minute. The fella upstairs said he wanted to kill you, Mr. Penlin told him to stand down until he arrived, and that was it."

"I need to make a call and find out who this Mr. Penlin is," Michelle told Mitchel. "Is there a private phone I can use?"

"There's a private phone located in my apartment," Mitchel explained and pointed to a wooden door behind the front desk. "Go through that door, walk down a short hallway, and take a left into my kitchen. The phone is hanging next to the refrigerator."

Michelle handed Sam her gun. "Sam, stay alert until I get back. Able, honey, please come with me." Able nodded his head and followed Michelle into Mitchel's apartment, feeling worried and uncertain. All he wanted to do was throw Michelle, Momma Peach, and Sam into the minivan and get out of town. Hanging around with a killer on the loose wasn't his idea of a fun vacation.

Sam glanced toward the staircase. "I saw that man back down the road by your brother's store. He sped past the store, sat a minute on the side of the road like he was looking at something, and then sped off. I should have said something, but...well, a part of me was just hoping for the best. Mighty stupid of me."

Momma Peach heard footsteps coming down the stairs and spotted Marc. Marc was carrying his fishing pole again. He looked at Momma Peach and Sam with hard eyes. Sam made no attempt to hide the gun he was holding. Marc honed in on the gun but still walked over to the front door and yanked it open. "You can't hunt bears with that pop gun," he said over his shoulder.

"I ain't hunting bears," Sam warned Marc.

Marc paused in the doorway, turned, and looked at Sam. He saw an old timer who wasn't afraid to stand up and fight, and that was a problem; deep down, it scared Marc. He projected his air of cruelty with precision and skill— yet inside, he was the kind of coward who felt helpless without a gun. Sure, he'd had his share of brawls throughout the years, but it wasn't until he became a skilled marksman that he began to take down his enemies in earnest. A gun killed—even a hard fist simply hurt. But he could see that Sam wasn't afraid of a gun or a hard fist. Sam was a fighter who wouldn't stop throwing his punches until he was dead. Marc would have to plan carefully to take down a man like that. "You better be sure of that, old man," Marc told Sam and walked outside.

"I would call the sheriff and make that man leave my lodge, but that might cause trouble," Mitchel worried. "Besides, the sheriff isn't the type of man to handle a dangerous situation calmly. That man would throw more gas on the fire than water."

"Best to leave the sheriff alone, Mr. Mitchel," Momma Peach told him. She walked over to the front window, pulled back a heavy curtain, and watched Marc head down a trail leading down to the lake. If he took the entire five-mile loop, he wouldn't be back until night had settled in over the lodge. "I fear that snake is going hunting for a burial spot so he can throw all of us in."

Sam looked at Mitchel. "Where do you keep your rifles?"

"In my apartment, where else," Mitchel told Sam in a calm voice. "I also have three handguns. I keep one handgun in my truck, one next to my bed, and one out in my work shed. During the warm months when I tend to the trails, I carry a rifle and my gun. My rifle handles any unwanted bears and my gun handles any unwanted snakes."

"How many rifles do you have?" Sam asked.

"Three. Two for hunting and one for bird hunting."

"Good," Sam said and looked at Momma Peach. "When this Mr. Penlin gets here, things could turn real ugly. Marc knows we're armed. He ain't gonna walk back in here dumb and stupid. He's out there wandering around making himself a plan of some sort."

"But Mr. Penlin ordered him to stand down," Michel told Sam. "I heard those very words with my own ears."

"I'm sure you did," Sam assured Mitchel, "but that doesn't mean this Mr. Penlin might not have a change of heart. And it doesn't mean that Marc will obey. He could be outside walking around because he knows his boss might have a change of plan and he wants to make sure he's ready for action when Penlin gets here."

Momma Peach felt scared, but she didn't show it. What Sam was stating was speculative, yet it had the ring of truth. She trusted Sam and knew he was a solid man to rely on. "Could be that snake outside is also thinking of a way to get rid of his boss?" she added and thought of the box of matches. "I will be right back, Mr. Sam. Stay put with Mr. Mitchel."

"Where are you going?" Sam asked.

"To get some toilet paper," Momma Peach said. She handed Sam her pocketbook and got her short little legs moving and hurried upstairs. When she reached her room, she saw her door standing open. "Oh, give me strength," she said and peeked into the room. The room seemed in order, but Momma Peach knew Marc had trespassed and snooped around, and it was like she could feel the chill of his glare lingering in the room. "What a vacation," Momma Peach said, and bravely stepped into her room and closed the door. A note was sitting on her bed. Momma Peach eased over to the bed and carefully picked up the note and read it: "Slide the matches under my room door and we're square. You have until dark."

Momma Peach folded the note up, hurried into the bathroom, grabbed the roll of toilet paper she had hidden the matchbox in, and hustled back downstairs. As she maneuvered down the hallway, her mind began to think about the man who had been found dead on the North Queen not so long ago, and about the mysterious timing of the recent fire. It seemed to her that she was involved in more than just a simple arson case. Momma Peach knew she was involved in a very dangerous murder case, and somehow this matchbox was the connection between the two.

Mitchel spotted Momma Peach working her way down the stairs. There was something special about the woman, he thought to himself; something very special. Momma Peach was a woman that made the world a far better place to live in, that was for sure. "What do you have in your hand, Momma Peach?" he asked.

Momma Peach walked up to the front counter and laid down the box of matches. "This here box of matches fell out of my rain jacket upstairs."

Sam picked up the box of matches. "Lake View Motel?" he asked. "Can't say I've ever stayed at that hotel."

"There's a far cry between a hotel and motel," Mitchel told Sam. "The hotels you see today are fancy and clean, modern and expensive. There are big national chain motels today that are clean and modern enough, too. But your average little roadside place like the Lake View Motel? It's cheap, dirty and run-down, like a grimy old sponge. Back in the old days those little motels were okay, but today most of them are places where the worst of society goes when they need to spend a night."

"Don't I know it, baby," Momma Peach said. She thought back to the run-down hotel in her home town and shook her head. "A killer who is trying to keep a low profile would stay at a cheap motel, too. I think these matches belong to that snake outside. I think he slid these matches into my jacket pocket when he bumped into me back in Seattle. I also think these here matches were used to set the kitchen on fire on that doomed ship, too. And last but not least, oh give me the strength, I think that snake followed me up here to Alaska to retrieve the matches or kill me trying."

Sam pulled open the box of matches and studied the contents. "Hey, will you look at this," he said.

Momma Peach stepped close to Sam. Mitchel peered his head over the front counter. "A key?" Mitchel asked, confused.

Sam held up a silver key in his right hand. "Any thoughts, Momma Peach?"

Momma Peach stared at the key. "I would bet my bakery that key will unlock one of the kitchen doors on the North Queen, yes, sir and yes ma'am." Momma Peach narrowed her eyes. "The snake outside felt some heat and got rid of the key. But...there has to be more. Mr. Sam, can I see the box?" Sam handed Momma Peach the box of matches. Momma Peach studied the box on every side, turning it carefully in her hands. "Ah," she said and pointed at the bottom of the matchbox, "there's some writing." Momma Peach held the box up to her eyes. "A phone number. We have a phone number, Mr. Sam." Momma Peach quickly memorized the phone number.

Sam took the box from Momma Peach and studied the phone number. "That's a Los Angeles area code, Momma Peach," he pointed out.

"Mr. Mitchel, may I use your phone for a second?" Momma Peach asked. "I need to make a long-distance phone call."

Mitchel nodded his head and retrieved the front desk phone and placed it down on the front counter. "Better hurry. No telling when that man will walk back in."

Momma Peach picked up the phone and dialed the Los Angeles number. "Hello, thank you for calling the Blue Wave cruise line. If you have reached this recording, our office is currently closed and will reopen at nine o'clock. If you wish to leave a message, please punch in the last three letters of the last name of the person you wish to reach." Momma Peach hung up the phone and rubbed her chin.

"Hey, look at this," Sam said and pointed at the matchbox. He squinted and focused on three letters. "I...can barely make out...three letters written under the phone number...the letters are very small...kinda faded."

"Let me see," Mitchel told Sam. Sam handed Mitchel the matchbox. Mitchel held the matchbox under the bright desk lamp to get a closer look and found the three letters and zoomed in on them. "Let's see what we have...the letter P...the letter E...and the letter N...PEN."

"The first three letters in the last name of the person you're trying to reach?" Momma Peach said to Sam and Mitchel.

"If you're trying to reach Penlin, I can tell you what his voicemail will say," said Michelle, looking through the doorway into the lobby with a worried look.

"What did you find out, baby?" Momma Peach said.

"This Mr. Penlin is the president of the Blue Wave cruise line company. I'll have more details in a moment...I'm on hold with my contact back at the station." Michelle disappeared back into the apartment doorway.

Momma Peach looked at Sam and Mitchel. "Goodness, we're now up to our necks in some serious trouble. Mr. Sam, maybe you better ask Mr. Mitchel if he will let you carry one of his guns on you."

Sam looked at Mitchel with worried eyes. Mitchel nodded his head. Yes, he knew the lodge was now in some very serious trouble. "Your reflexes are probably far better than mine," Mitchel told Sam. "A man hates to admit when his reflexes are slowing down, but right now ain't no time for my pride to be worrying about itself."

Sam nodded his head. He respected Mitchel and the respect he felt for the man was growing by the second. "Okay, Momma Peach," he said, "what are you thinking?"

"I'm thinking a lot of money is involved," Momma Peach stated. She rubbed her chin and began pacing around in a small circle. "Mr. Penlin of the Blue Wave cruise line company is about to pay us a visit, Mr. Sam. That man ain't coming all this way to shake our hands. And we have to remember, Mr. Callahan Minson was found dead on the North Queen. Mr. Minson, according to Michelle, was interested in buying the North Queen."

"So why would Penlin kill the man?" Sam asked. He

watched Momma Peach as her short little legs walked her around and around in a circle.

"It could be, Mr. Sam, that Mr. Minson wasn't who he appeared to be," Momma Peach explained. "And if Mr. Minson wasn't who he was claiming to be, maybe Mr. Penlin decided it was better to drown the poor man, rest his soul. Yes, sir and yes ma'am. Murder is surely awful."

Sam leaned against the front counter and glanced anxiously at the front door. "So here is what we know," he said in a careful voice. "It seems like that snake outside set the kitchen on the North Queen on fire before the ship could head out to sea. It also seems like this Mr. Penlin fella ordered the fire, if he's Marc's boss. Am I walking in the right direction, Momma Peach?"

"You sure are, baby."

Sam nodded his head. "Penlin's hired arsonist then slipped the matches he used to set the fire on the North Queen into the pocket of your rain jacket. Why? Panic? Maybe he was being followed? But after looking that man in the eyes, the only reason I can guess he ditched those matches would be because he was being followed by someone...a cop...Penlin himself trying to turn him in...a private investigator...who knows? But someone made that man nervous enough to force him to get rid of the box of matches he had in his possession."

"Momma Peach agrees, baby," Momma Peach told Sam.

She stopped pacing and looked at the front door. "Mr. Sam, Mr. Mitchel, sometimes the boss kills off an employee who becomes a threat. Could it be that Mr. Penlin is coming here to kill that snake slithering around outside? And...kill us, too? Could it be," Momma Peach said in a worried voice, "that Mr. Penlin isn't going to arrive alone?"

Sam felt a hard chill run down his spine. Mitchel drew in a deep breath. Oh yes, the lodge was definitely in a heap of trouble.

Michelle and Able walked back into the front lobby. Michelle's face was worried. "I made a few calls and was able to create a profile on Mr. Penlin," she said.

Sam handed Michelle back her gun. "The man upstairs came down and went outside right after you and Able went into Mitchel's apartment to use the phone. We don't know when he'll be back."

Michelle looked over at the front door. "I'll be quick, then," she said and focused back on the topic at hand. "Mr. Heath Penlin, aged forty-eight, six foot one, one hundred and seventy-five pounds. He's unmarried, no children, currently living in Seattle, and currently President of the Blue Wave cruise line company. He has been president since his sister, Wilma Penlin, was found drowned in her bathtub. The woman's death was apparently ruled a suicide."

Momma Peach touched her heart and shook her head. "My, my, people sure seem to be taking deadly swims when that man is around. Yes, sir and yes ma'am."

Michelle nodded her head in agreement and continued. "Heath Penlin spent twenty years in prison for robbing a bank in Los Angeles. He got out of prison four years ago." Michelle glanced around at the faces staring at her in shock. "Two people and a cop were killed during the bank robbery. Heath Penlin took a bullet to his shoulder. His partner in crime got away with the money."

"And he only served twenty years?" Mitchel asked in a shocked voice.

"That's the justice system for you," Michelle said in a disgusted voice. "Heath Penlin's parents hired the best law firm in California. The law firm managed to cut a deal in exchange for his testimony: twenty years instead of life." Michelle bit down on her lower lip. "Heath Penlin's parents are both dead. They left Wilma Penlin the Blue Wave cruise line, which at the time of their death was called the Deep Treasure cruise line company. Heath Penlin renamed the company to its current name."

"Keep going, baby," Momma Peach told Michelle, keeping a careful eye on the front door.

"Apparently Wilma Penlin was struggling financially

when she allowed her brother to join the cruise line company. Otherwise she would never have let a convicted felon help run the business. She was close to filing for bankruptcy. The financial troubles for the cruise line began shortly after Wilma Penlin purchased the North Queen from a cruise company in France that was being forced to shut down for numerous code violations."

"Ms. Wilma Penlin bought herself a lemon," Momma Peach told Michelle.

"It looks that way," Michelle replied. "There are five cruise ships belonging to the Blue Wave cruise line company. Two of the ships run routes to the Caribbean islands, two ships to Mexico, and the last ship, the North Queen, was purchased to make runs to Alaska. Now, I'm sure everyone standing in this room understands how packed the seas are with ships sailing to the Caribbean and to Mexico."

"Elbow to elbow," Able stated.

"And each year more modern cruise ships are being built, equipped with the very best a cruise line can offer...larger cabins, more shows, pools, theaters, games, activities, the works."

"Imagine going from an old sailboat to a yacht," Able finished for Michelle. "Each ship belonging to the Blue Wave cruise line is an old sailboat, outdated and rusted when compared to the new Porsches sailing the open seas."

"But..." Momma Peach said, knowing that was not the end of the story.

"But," Michelle continued and tossed a sweet, caring smile at Able, "the North Queen isn't exactly a rusted old sailboat. Sure, the ship is a lemon, but that ship is a pretty lemon filled with better facilities than her sister ships. For instance, the private gym Mr. Minson was found dead in is a new addition. Also, the North Queen has a private dining hall reserved for passengers who are rich enough to swim in cash."

"Don't forget the private hallways," Able added.

"Oh, yeah," Michelle said, "the North Queen also features private hallways that separate the rich passengers from the regular passengers."

"And the ship also had a private cigar lounge and a tea room for the ladies," Able added.

"While at the same time, it added in some extra features for passengers, such as a water slide park for the kids, a movie theater, an arcade, broader menu options, a clothing shop...nice stuff," Michelle confessed. "It was, after all, why we were so excited when you won those tickets, Momma Peach."

Momma Peach rubbed her chin again. "Now, why would

Ms. Penlin dish out so much money on a lemon?" she asked herself. "Why not fancy up one of her other cruise ships, if she was so close to bankruptcy?"

"The renovations on the North Queen didn't begin until after Heath Penlin was brought on board," Michelle told Momma Peach. "Shortly after, the woman was found dead."

"Could be that Wilma Penlin didn't tell her brother the North Queen was a lemon?" Sam suggested.

"Lemon or not, that ship is cursed and gives me the willies," Momma Peach told Sam. She cradled her arms together and shivered. "Is it getting cold in here to y'all?"

Michelle walked over and placed her arm around Momma Peach. "The North Queen didn't sit well with me, either, Momma Peach," she confessed. "At least now we know why."

Able watched Michelle comfort Momma Peach. He saw a tenderness in the woman that captured his heart. Sure, Michelle could tangle with a wild tiger if the situation called for it, but she has a tender heart and a soft soul that only wanted to be loved in return. He wanted desperately to protect her. "I suggest we leave," Able turned and looked at Mitchel. "You, too, sir."

"I don't run from a fight, son," Mitchel informed Able. "This is my lodge. My wife and I spent many good years here together. I would rather die defending what we created hand-in-hand than run like a coward. I know you can't understand what I'm saying to you now, but maybe," Mitchel nodded at Michelle, "someday you will."

Able looked back at Michelle. He saw a beauty in her face that set his heart on fire. "Maybe," he said in a hopeful voice.

"We couldn't leave if we wanted to," Sam told Able. "If we did, I think that snake outside would jump in his truck and chase us down. Even if we disabled his truck and scrammed, we would always be looking over our shoulders, examining every shadow, questioning every face. It's better if we stay and fight it out. Are you with me?"

Michelle looked at Able with hopeful eyes. Her new boyfriend was now being put to the ultimate test and she wanted to see if he would cower or stand up like a man. Of course, she felt in her heart that Able would stand up like a man. Able wasn't a coward. "Well," Able said and pushed his glasses up on his pointed nose, "I never did like bullies and I sure don't want to go through the rest of my life looking over my shoulder. I stated the obvious, but sometimes the obvious can be the wrong choice to take. We're staying."

Michelle smiled. "Isn't he wonderful?" she whispered in Momma Peach's ear.

"He sure is, baby," Momma Peach replied. Able looked at

the front door and started to walk over to it, but then tripped over an untied shoe lace and toppled down onto the floor. "A bit clumsy, but wonderful."

"Darn shoelace," Able fussed.

Sam reached down and pulled Able up to his feet. "Easy, cowboy," he grinned, "no sense in blaming the horse for bucking at your boot spur."

"I guess," Able sighed and brushed off his knees. He looked at Michelle and blushed.

Michelle smiled at Able. "My hero," she said.

The lobby grew quiet. No one spoke for a few minutes. Everyone stared at the front door wondering what to expect. Momma Peach knew trouble was coming. She also knew that if she ran, trouble would follow her all the way back to Georgia, straight back to her hometown and straight into the kitchen of her bakery. She had Mandy and Rosa—and even Old Joe—to think about. And what if she just up and left poor Mr. Mitchel? Surely the nice man would end up floating face down in the beautiful lake outside, turning the lake into a watery horror scene. No, it was best to stay and fight it out, as Mr. Sam and Mr. Mitchel said. Besides, Momma Peach thought, staring at the front door, it seemed to her that one snake was arriving to kill off another snake and maybe that was for the best. Dealing with one snake at a time was surely better than dealing with two. But then again, Momma

Peach reminded herself, maybe the larger snake that was on his way might be arriving in a dark SUV packed with other snakes? Time would surely tell.

"Well," Momma Peach said, "ain't no sense in standing around feeling all hungry. Mr. Sam, you go with Mr. Mitchel and get yourself a gun. Michelle, baby, you stand here with Able and watch the lobby. I will go find myself the kitchen and prepare everyone some food. Yes, sir and yes ma'am, ain't no sense in thinking on a hungry belly. A hungry belly drains the brain. Oh, give me strength. But before we eat," Momma Peach showed Michelle the box of matches and pointed out the phone number and the three letters written on the matchbox, "baby, you better examine this."

Michelle took the matchbox and examined the phone number and three letters. "P...E...N," she read the letters out loud. "This is where you found the letters I heard you talking about before. P-E-N for Penlin?"

"That's right, baby. And when I called the number scribbled inside this matchbox I got the Blue Wave cruise line's after hours answering service."

"Where did you get this matchbox?" Michelle asked.

Momma Peach hesitated. "Well, baby, it seems that awful man outside slid the matchbox into the pocket of my rain jacket back down there in Seattle when he bumped into me. Now," Momma Peach held up her hands, "before you get all mad at me for not saying so earlier, let me just tell you that I found that box of matches not more than an hour ago when I was unpacking. That box of matches just went and dropped right out of the pocket of my rain jacket as easy as butter sliding off a hot plate. It was right before I came out and that awful man started menacing me in the hallway. Yes, sir and yes ma'am."

"You could have told me then, Momma Peach," Michelle said in a hurt voice. "We're partners. We never hide anything from each other."

Momma Peach lowered her eyes, looked down, shifted from one foot to another, and then looked back up at Michelle. "You're so happy, baby," she said in a soft voice. "I ain't never seen you so happy before." Momma Peach pointed at Able. "That man is making your heart sing with joy and you're making his heart sing right back, yes, sir and yes ma'am, you sure are. Maybe I hoped to get some time to think and work through some thoughts before worrying you. I was hoping to get through supper time before ruining your good time. But then that snake slithered up to me outside of my room and started making a scene."

Michelle stared into Momma Peach's loving eyes. She knew Momma Peach had kept the box of matches secret in order to protect her emotions. "Thank you, Momma Peach. I know you care deeply about me, and I love you to pieces. But I'm a cop first."

"I know, baby," Momma Peach told Michelle. "And honey...Detective Chan, I have something else to confess. The awful man broke into my room and left a note on my bed. It said if I slide that there box of matches under his door then he'll leave me alone. If not...then it's lights out. Now, I know I ain't gonna be square with the house if I toss that box of matches under a door, no, sir and no ma'am. I just needed some time to chew on a few ideas."

"Momma Peach, you should have told us," Sam said, upset. "Your life is in danger here."

"I know that my life is in danger. I also know that every life standing in this room is in danger, too, Mr. Sam. I love Michelle and Able and Mr. Sam and now Mr. Mitchel too, and I don't want anything to happen to you. I like to think matters through a bit before serving them up on a platter." Momma Peach picked her pocketbook up off the front counter. "Everyone standing in this room is my family and I am going to protect you all. So fuss at me if you want, but I needed time for my mind to chew on some thoughts."

"I'm not fussing," Sam told Momma Peach. He wrapped his arm around her. "I'm worried for you, that's all. Momma Peach, you've become my family, too. If anything happened to you I would never forgive myself. So from this point forward, I'm your shadow."

Momma Peach looked up into Sam's worried and caring eyes. She saw a good man staring down at her—a man with an honest heart and brave soul. "That snake outside will come back after dark, Mr. Sam. We have to be ready for him."

"When is Mr. Penlin due to arrive?" Sam asked Mitchel.

Mitchel scratched the back of his head. "By midnight, or so he said. He was pretending to be a photographer who wanted to come up my way and snap a few photos, but I knew better."

"A photographer?" Momma Peach asked.

"That must mean Mr. Penlin wants to keep his identity a secret," Michelle stated. She focused on Mitchel. "What name did Penlin use to make the reservation?"

Mitchel scratched the back of his neck again. "I guess I should have given out this information earlier. My mind is worried, that's all. I'd hate to see anything happen to my lodge. My wife and me, we sure put some good years into this place. I can still see my wife now...walking up the stairs, carrying fresh towels up to the rooms. Oh, she was a stickler about the rooms being clean and tidy. Not a drop of dust on her watch."

Momma Peach saw pain and sorrow grip Mitchel's eyes. "I'm sorry, honey."

"So am I," Mitchel said with a heavy sadness. "Uh...where was I? Oh, the name...Mr. Penlin made the reservation under the name William Smith."

"Creative," Michelle rolled her eyes.

Momma Peach fished a piece of peppermint out of her pocketbook and placed it into her mouth. "Baby, I recommend we treat Mr. William Smith like any old ordinary fella. As a matter of fact," Momma Peach added, "I'm going to slide that there box of matches under the door of that ugly man Marc and see how he reacts."

"What you're saying is that we don't need to let on that we know that Mr. Smith is Mr. Penlin and by doing so we could possibly have a hand up in the matter, right?" Able asked Momma Peach.

Momma Peach walked over and kissed Able on his cheek. "Baby, I love your brain," she said and then asked Mitchel to show her the kitchen. "My belly is hungry and I'm ready to eat. Oh, give me strength, give me the strength to get through this night."

CHAPTER FOUR

"**W**hat do you think is going to happen?" Able asked Michelle.

Michelle eased open the front door and peered out into a darkening evening, studying the lush, breathtaking landscape of evergreens on the hills surrounding the lake, and then eased the door closed. "So beautiful," she sighed. "We should be outside right now, preparing a campfire down next to the lake. Instead, we're caught up in another case. Sometimes...oh, forget it," Michelle said.

"Sometimes what?" Able asked Michelle.

Michelle shrugged her shoulders. "Able, I love being a cop. Being a cop is who I am. But sometimes I wonder...if it's time for a change? I kinda overheard Sam telling Momma Peach that he's going to buy this lodge when Mitchel decides to sell it."

"Sell it? That man's life is carved into every log in this lodge," Able said in a shocked voice.

"I guess in time, when he becomes too old to manage this lodge, he'll pass it on to someone he knows will care for it and love it the same as he and his wife did," Michelle explained.

Able stared at Michelle. "Are you saying you want to move to Alaska and live in this lodge?"

"That thought did...kinda...cross my mind," Michelle winced. "Sam told Momma Peach this lodge will belong to us as well as him. He wants us to travel to Alaska and help him manage the lodge. Oh, not year-round of course. Sam knows Momma Peach has her bakery to run and I could never move away from Momma Peach myself...but...maybe it would be nice to have a place of our own to escape to every now and then."

Able didn't know what to say. He did like the lodge. As a matter of fact, he loved the lodge. He loved the feel, the smell, the taste of winter in the air, the smell of chimney smoke, the lake, the trees, the land, everything. But he could never leave his mother. Not that he was a momma's boy—far from it. "You know, my mother is growing older and I want to spend more time with her and make up for the years I lost living in Philadelphia. That's partly why I came back to Georgia, as you know. But...living in Alaska a few months out of the year surely wouldn't hurt. As a matter of fact, the thought of living in Alaska a few months out of the year sounds...healthy and exciting. Like something that can truly be ours. Count me in," he smiled.

"Really?" Michelle asked, shocked.

Able nodded his head. "Yes," he promised. "Michelle, I left Philadelphia after I lost my job, discouraged and down-hearted, unsure about my future and what path to take. But now, here I am standing in this lodge with the most beautiful woman in the world, feeling alive for the first time in a very long time. I spent too many years sitting behind a desk and living in a cramped little apartment, hunkered down, hoping for the best, and not doing, well...anything to make the situation better. The only reason I even moved to Philadelphia was to prove to my dad that I...wasn't the...wimp he always accused me of being." He looked away, as if embarrassed to admit this.

"Your dad called you a wimp?" Michelle asked. She felt her temper rise.

Able shrugged his shoulders. "My dad was a tough, no-nonsense businessman. Everything was black and white to him, no gray zone." Able bit down on his lower lip. "I was always...well, a sickly child growing up, which didn't sit well with my dad. He wanted a tough son who played sports and had girls lined up for dates practically every night of the week. Me...I couldn't get a date to save my life and instead of playing sports...I wrote stories. My dad didn't like me writing stories. Stories were a waste of time and mental energy to him. My mother," Able sighed, "always defended me. She and dad...they would get into these awful yelling fights over me."

"I'm sorry."

"Don't be," Able told Michelle. "I'm not. My dad died regretting the day I was born. I lived trying to prove myself to him. In the end, we both lost. The war is over. Dad is dead and I'm here with you. And...well, I don't want to have to enter another war and try to prove myself to you. I want you to accept me for who I am and what I am."

"I do," Michelle promised. She reached out and softly touched Able's cheek. "Honey, I do accept you for who and what you are."

"I know," Able blushed and looked down at the floor. "And that's the miracle. Now...I can be myself and take a chance at...being happy." Michelle stepped closer so he had no choice but to hold her in his arms, and then gently kissed him. "What was that for?" Able asked, staring into Michelle's sparkling brown eyes.

"For being you," Michelle smiled. "Able, Momma Peach loves me for who I am. I love her for who she is. Is Momma Peach perfect? Oh, no. You should hear that woman fussing when she accidentally burns one of her peach pies. Everyone in Georgia can hear Momma Peach fussing when she burns a pie. And you better stay away from her when she gets in the mood to try a new recipe." Michelle giggled. "That woman goes insane until she gets the recipe just right. Even Mandy and Rosa know to run. And that's okay, because Momma Peach has a heart of gold. She would lay down her life for you, Able, without blinking an eye."

"I can see that."

Michelle nodded her head. "And what about me? There are days when I'm as cranky as a rattlesnake until I get my first cup of coffee and powdered donut down." Michelle took Able's left hand. "Able, what I'm trying to tell you is that no one in the world is perfect. We love each other through the good and the bad. If all people want from you is the good and refuse to accept the bad, then those people aren't true friends."

"I...snore," Able confessed.

"So do I," Michelle grinned.

"Really?"

"Like a log. Well, according to Momma Peach," Michelle laughed. "Momma Peach doesn't lie, either."

Able felt a tender hand touch his heart. "So...you accept me for my good and bad qualities?"

Michelle nodded her head. "And I can look into your eyes and tell that you will accept me for my grumpy side in the morning and my good side after the coffee sets in."

"Coffee...I might want to make a mental note of that," Able replied and brought Michelle into another soft embrace. "Yes, I will definitely need to make a mental note about the coffee."

Mitchel walked back into the lobby and watched Able hug Michelle. He smiled and wondered from behind the front counter. "Love is in the air," he began to sing.

"Oh," Michelle jumped and let go of Able, blushing like a schoolgirl caught kissing behind a locker door. "We didn't see you come in."

"My wife always told people that I walk like a fox," Mitchel grinned at Michelle. "Relax, young lady, you aren't doing anything wrong. That's the natural way of love between a good man and good woman." Mitchel pointed at Able. "You're a decent fella, I can tell. You'll make a good husband for this young woman."

Able blushed. "I...well, what I mean to say is...the thought of marriage...I mean..."

Mitchel grinned. "I know exactly what you're trying to say, son. I stood in your very shoes years ago when my wife's father asked me if I was intending on marrying his daughter. So take a deep breath and relax."

"Speaking of relaxing," Michelle said, quickly changing the subject, "that man Marc is still outside and the sun is setting."

Mitchel looked at the front door. "Go lock the door, please," he said. "I always lock the front door. There's a sign posted out on the front porch stating the door is locked when the sun sets."

Michelle quickly locked the front door. "Should I go and lock any more downstairs doors?" she asked.

"My apartment door is locked. The kitchen door is locked. The emergency exit door is locked from the outside. The basement door is locked. And now the front door is locked. I guess that'll about do it," Mitchel told Michelle in a relieved voice. "Each door has a solid deadbolt that can hold back a bear, and they're all like this front door—made of the finest, heaviest wood. If that man outside wants to get in, he's going to have to ring the outside bell."

"I checked the guest registry," Michelle said. "Marc signed in as 'Charlie Jones.' At least I have a handwriting sample. And later on, whenever I can get to the local police station, I'll grab a fingerprint kit and come back to the lodge and grab a few of his fingerprints and find out what his record is. We may know his name, but we need to know who he really is."

"Men like that..." Mitchel said and grimaced as if he had a bad taste in his mouth. "Nah, I don't want to know who he is. A dead snake is the best snake. And speaking of a snake," Mitchel said and glanced toward the door leading back into the kitchen, "I guess I better get the guest registry form out for the man arriving tonight. Momma Peach wants the lobby to appear as normal as possible when Mr. Penlin arrives...or, Mr. William Smith. Guess I better make sure I call the man by the name he made the reservation under and not slip up and say his real name."

"You'll be fine," Michelle assured Mitchel.

Able glanced at the fireplace. "Mind if I add some more logs to the fire?" he asked Mitchel. "Air in here is getting a bit chilly."

"Go right ahead, son."

Able walked over to a log bin, fished out two healthy logs, and carefully placed the logs down onto the fire. Sparks shot up from the small fire burning in the fireplace. The fire was nearly out, but Able knew there was enough fire and heat left to burn the new, larger logs. Soon the small fire would grow into a large, strong fire, warm enough to battle the cold of the night. "Love the smell of a fireplace," he told Michelle and brushed some bark off his hands.

"Me too," Michelle said. She walked over to the fireplace and warmed her hands. No matter how warm a summer was in Alaska, she felt that the bite of winter never fully left the air. The heart of winter settled into the land and remained year-round, hidden at times, but very much alive. The thought of winter made Michelle feel cozy inside. She looked at the coffee pot warming on a hook over the fire and smiled. Four brown coffee mugs were sitting on a stone mantle above the fireplace. Michelle grabbed a mug. "Mitchel, how strong is your coffee?"

"Strong enough to wake a bear from hibernation," Mitchel told Michelle. "That coffee has been warming over the fire for a few hours now. Should be just about right by now." Mitchel walked out from behind the front counter, made his way over to the fireplace, grabbed a thick green oven mitten off the stone mantle, and carefully took the coffee pot from the metal hook hanging over the fire. "Allow an old man to pour you a cup of coffee," he told Michelle.

"I'd be honored," Michelle smiled. She raised the mug up to Mitchel and watched him pour coffee into it. "Smells delicious," she said and carefully took a sip. "Whoa..." She coughed. "It is strong."

Mitchel smiled proudly. "Up here in Alaska we drink coffee the right way." Mitchel looked at Able. "Son, want a cup?"

"Uh...maybe later," Able promised. Mitchel grinned again and replaced the coffee pot back onto the metal hook. "Coffee sure smells good, though."

"Coffee and winter are best friends," Mitchel explained. "A strong winter requires strong coffee. When the snow sets in, a man can't sip on a weak cup of coffee, son. Hard winters require hard men."

"I've been sitting behind a desk for years," Able said in a slightly bitter tone. "I'd probably get a blister shoveling snow."

Mitchel patted Able's shoulder. "The first blister is the best one," he smiled and walked back behind the front counter.

Able lifted his hands up to his face, examining them in the firelight. The sight of his soft hands brought back years of bad memories. How many meaningless hours had he spent behind a desk carrying out pointless tasks for people who made fun of him behind his back? "A blister sounds good," he said.

Mitchel nodded his head. "Son, you earn blisters through hard work. Hard work is good for a man. Keeps him alive and young. When a man sits down, he might as well die." Mitchel looked over to the front door. "Many a year I've walked out that door with a snow shovel in my hands," he continued. "Many a year I've shoveled off the front porch with an aching back and frozen hands. This year won't be any different, either. And that's just how I want things, son. I want the good Lord to keep my old body challenged with honest chores. I want to shovel snow off my front porch and chop wood...even be it with my chainsaw more than my axe, now that I'm getting on up in years." Mitchel nodded his head. "The land up here in Alaska is unforgiving and deadly, as well as beautiful and alluring. The land will be good to you once you learn to respect it. Honest men make it up here. Cowards die off."

Michelle took a careful sip of her coffee and grew silent. Able lowered his hands and looked at the front door. They watched and waited, the tension unspoken as the logs in the fireplace crackled and flamed higher.

Outside, night was rapidly turning the land dark. Down by the lake, Marc stood silent on the edge of a trail, staring up at the lodge with poisonous fury. He raised his binoculars to check the lodge's entrance road but saw no headlights just yet. He chuckled, welcoming the cold of the night because it suited the deadly certainty he felt in his gut. "Soon you will all die, including you, Penlin."

Sam leaned against a wooden counter and studied the kitchen of the lodge. The kitchen wasn't big or small—it was comfortable and cozy. The walls were made of smoothed logs and the floor was polished hardwood. Hand-carved wooden cabinets hung on the walls, old and aged. Sam liked the cabinets. He also liked the wood stove sitting in the middle of the kitchen; even though the kitchen was equipped with a modern stove, too. "Smell the air in here," he said to Momma Peach and drew in a deep breath. "It smells like...woodsmoke...coffee...and cinnamon...it's winter...all mixed in together."

"I like the smell in the air too, baby," Momma Peach told Sam, standing before a sink filled with supper dishes. "How was supper?"

"Great, just great," Sam smiled. "And the peach pie you made...well, my stomach will sleep well tonight." Sam picked up a red checkered dish towel and waited for Momma Peach to hand him a plate to dry. "I guess it won't be long before Penlin shows up. I'm glad my stomach will be operating on full instead of empty."

"I am glad, too," Momma Peach told Sam. She stopped washing the brown plate in her hands and looked out of an oval window above the sink. The oval window faced toward the woods. For a few seconds, Momma Peach imagined it snowing outside. She imagined a pot of coffee brewing on the old wooden stove standing behind her. She imagined peach bread baking in the oven. And for a few seconds, Momma Peach forgot all about her troubles. "Mr. Sam?"

"Yes, Momma Peach?"

"You really want to buy this lodge?" Momma Peach asked in a wistful voice.

Sam looked into Momma Peach's sweet face. "Yes, Momma Peach, I do."

"I want you to buy this lodge, too," Momma Peach smiled. She glanced up at Sam. "I feel very cozy in this lodge."

Sam smiled. "Me, too," he confessed. "I know a lot of hard work goes into maintaining this place. I don't mind hard work, Momma Peach. Hard work produces good fruit."

Momma Peach patted Sam's right arm with a hand covered with dish suds. "I like hard work, too, baby." Momma Peach looked back at the oval window. "I want to ice skate on the lake when it freezes over. Oh, sure, I will fall down a few times and bruise my tender backside, but so what? And oh, when it snows, I will bake peach bread and make coffee and sit around the fireplace with my precious family and talk the night through. Yes, sir and yes ma'am, some good times are coming."

"Sounds wonderful," Sam told Momma Peach in a hopeful voice. "I can just see us sitting in front of the fireplace drinking coffee, eating your peach bread, and talking through a snow storm." Sam closed his eyes and saw Momma Peach carrying a plate full of peach bread into the lobby. "My mouth is watering right now."

Momma Peach stared up into Sam's face. She sure was fond of Sam. Not romantically, of course—her heart belonged to her husband who was waiting for her in heaven. The way she felt toward Sam was special; deep and powerful. It was as she had somehow known Sam her entire life and now the man had entered her life and she was being given permission to make up for lost times. Sam felt like a close, dear, loving friend who warmed her heart in places that not even Michelle could reach. "You're very special to me, Mr. Sam."

Sam opened his eyes, looked down at Momma Peach, and smiled. "So are you," he promised. "Who else can make peach bread the way you do?"

"No one, baby, and don't you ever forget it! Oh yes, sir and yes ma'am, I get crazy in my kitchen! Oh, give me strength! Alaska won't know what's hit 'em when Momma Peach comes to town," Momma Peach chuckled and went back to washing the dishes. "Give me strength, indeed."

"And give me a bigger belt," Sam chuckled back. Momma Peach shot Sam a wink and handed him a plate. Sam took the plate and began drying it. "I don't expect Mitchel to sell anytime soon. He's pushing up in years but he still has a few good leaps left in his legs. I'll make visits up here to see him and learn the layout of the land, how to manage the lodge, learn the weather, stuff like that."

Momma Peach nodded her head. "You will be an expert by the time you buy this lodge."

Sam placed the plate he was drying down into the dish drainer on the counter. "Speaking of buying," he told Momma Peach, "I wonder when Able and Michelle are going to tie the knot? When they do, I want to buy them a house. Now, before you say no, I've already settled my mind on the matter."

Momma Peach grabbed another plate and began scrubbing it. "I wasn't going to say a word, baby," she told Sam and began whistling. "No, sir and no ma'am, I wasn't going to say a word because I'm going to pay half for the house Michelle and her soon-to-be hubby choose."

Sam grinned. "You're a very sneaky woman, Momma Peach."

"And don't you ever forget it, Mr. Sam," Momma Peach grinned back. But then, all of a sudden, she became sad.

"Momma Peach?" Sam asked, watching the change come over her face. "What's the matter?"

"Oh," Momma Peach said. She stopped scrubbing the plate and looked out through the oval window. "Michelle won't have much time for me once she gets married. And we both know there's going to be a sweet, precious baby coming along soon after the wedding." Momma Peach sighed. "I am a sentimental old gal, Mr. Sam. I like for things to stay the same. I also know Michelle needs a husband and a family of her own, too. I'm being selfish by wanting to keep her baby all to myself."

"Not selfish," Sam objected. Sam put his hand on Momma Peach's shoulder. "I understand."

"You do?"

"Sure I do," Sam said and offered a kind smile. "Momma Peach, I was planning on dying in my town and being buried behind that old court house. I loved my town...that dusty, old, hot, run-down town was a part of me...and now it's gone. I spent a good portion of my life building that town up from the dirt. Sweat, blisters, aches, pains, sun burns through the roof," Sam sighed, "that town became me, and I became that town. I became part of the desert, too...and as strange as this might sound, I even started to depend on the desert to keep me safe."

"Safe?" Momma Peach asked. She looked away from the oval window and into Sam's eyes. "What do you mean by safe?"

Sam removed his hand from Momma Peach's shoulder and picked up a brown mug full of coffee. He took a sip of coffee and grew silent for a few seconds. "People are trouble, Momma Peach," he finally spoke in a tired voice, his voice roughened like the veteran cowboy he was. "People are trouble and they cause trouble. People also like to stay where they can be spoiled, too."

"You're talking about large cities?"

Sam nodded his head. "People like convenience, bright lights, air conditioning, cable television, hot water, modern day pampering, which means most of the troublemakers stay in larger cities and avoid a dusty, hot, small town roasting in the desert heat. Out there in the desert, I didn't turn on the television and hear about a killing, a fatal auto accident, a bank robbery, a gang fight, a gas station being robbed, none of that awful noise.

Instead of watching the six o'clock news, I was walking around my quiet little town in peace and solitude." Sam took another sip of his coffee. "The desert kept the people away—the bad people. Never once did I ever encounter a troublemaker in my town. Except in the end."

Momma Peach understood what Sam was getting at. "My kitchen is my desert, right Mr. Sam? And Michelle is my main ingredient."

Sam nodded his head. "I think so. But you also have Mandy and Rosa, who are both very sweet girls with good hearts and kind souls. But someday, Momma Peach, Mandy and Rosa are going to get married, too. Change is life's main ingredient sometimes. All we can do as old fogies is roll with the punches."

"Roll with a broken heart, you mean."

"No," Sam said in a soft, warm voice, "not a broken heart, Momma Peach. Sure, Michelle is going to marry Able. We can both see that. And someday, Mandy and Rosa are going to get married. But out of every new situation comes great things."

"Such as?"

"A sweet baby," Sam told Momma Peach and finished off his coffee. "Michelle is going to need a lot of help. That woman can kick my teeth out in a hand-to-hand fight, but I doubt she knows how to change a dirty diaper and warm a bottle." Momma Peach felt a smile touch her lips.

"And Able, oh boy Momma Peach, every time his baby cries that man is going to be running in every direction, tripping all over himself." Momma Peach's smile widened. "Your phone is going to be ringing off the hook. And it wouldn't surprise me one bit if Michelle asks you to move in with her and Able full time."

"Really?" Momma Peach asked as a tear rolled down her cheek.

Sam nodded his head. "Momma Peach, the future is always changing, but you better know that Michelle, Mandy, Rosa, Able and especially me, we're not letting you go and we pray you don't let us go, either."

Momma Peach burst out in tears, wrapped her arms around Sam, and hugged him. "I ain't ever gonna let go of my family...no, sir and no ma'am."

Sam wrapped his arms around Momma Peach. Momma Peach was something special. There wasn't another woman like her in all the world. "Now, tell me something," he said.

Momma Peach raised her teary eyes up to Sam. "What, baby?"

"Are you going to teach Michelle to change a dirty diaper or do I have to do it?"

Momma Peach wiped at her tears and chuckled to herself. "Baby, you better let me handle that department.

You can teach Able, bless his heart, how to put a crib together the right way. Oh, give me strength."

Momma Peach heard Michelle clear her throat from the kitchen doorway. She looked over and saw Michelle fold her arms together. "Able and I aren't married yet and you two are already planning the nursery for our first child?"

"You bet," Momma Peach beamed. She wiped at her tears and quickly went back to washing the supper dishes to hide her huge smile.

Sam cast an eye at Michelle and nodded at Momma Peach. Michelle understood. "I think I'll go stand watch in the lobby with Able and Mitchel," he said and left the kitchen.

Michelle walked over to Momma Peach, picked up the dish rag Sam was using to dry the dishes with and began twirling it in her hands. "I heard you and Sam talking."

"I know you did, baby. Here, dry this plate."

Michelle stopped twirling the dish rag and took the plate. "Momma Peach—"

"Honey, I was just being a sentimental old fool and—"

"Sam was right," Michelle told Momma Peach in a loving but firm tone. "When Able and I do get married someday and have a baby, I want you to live with us. Now, I know that's a long way away, but..." Michelle dried the plate and set it down in the drying rack, "I'm scared to go into the future without you," she confessed.

Momma Peach gave Michelle a confused expression. "You? Scared, baby? You can kick the fur off a grizzly bear."

Michelle shook her head. "I'm not that kind of scared," she explained. "I'm scared of...the unknown, Momma Peach. I want you at my side. If I don't have you, then...well, there's really no point in even facing the future. Do you remember when we first met?"

"I sure do, baby," Momma Peach said and gently touched Michelle's cheek. "You wouldn't speak two words to anyone. You were shy, lonely and very much hurt."

"No one tried to care, either...except you, Momma Peach. You took the time to care about me. You brought me lunch at work. You called me. You took me out to dinner. You came over to my house and watched movies with me. You helped me bake my first peach pie."

"Oh, give me strength, the fire department still tells stories about the fire you caused in my kitchen," Momma Peach exclaimed.

Michelle blushed. "I guess I kinda did cause...a little fire," she admitted and then made a pained face. "Okay, a large fire. Sorry about that, Momma Peach. But we did have fun putting up new wallpaper afterwards, didn't we?"

Momma Peach nodded her head. "We sure did, baby."

Michelle reached out and took Momma Peach's hands. "I'm falling in love with Able and I know he's falling in love with me. But we're both far from being ready to get married, Momma Peach. When the day arrives for us to say our vows in a lovely church, you'll be there. And when my first child arrives, you'll be there. You'll be there to see my child grow up, too." Michelle looked deep into Momma Peach's sweet eyes. "Don't you see, that, Momma Peach? As long as we're a family, we can face the future together."

Momma Peach broke out crying again. She pulled Michelle into her arms and held her. "Oh, my sweet baby."

Michelle began crying. "Look at us...two crying women in a kitchen, way out in the Alaska wilderness."

"As long as the grizzly bears don't see us, I don't care, baby," Momma Peach cried. She squeezed Michelle. "I will move in with you when the time comes and teach you how to change a dirty diaper and warm a bottle and deal with diaper rash and all that good stuff, I promise. But please, baby, oh please, give me a room far away from yours because as much as I love you...you snore! Oh, give me strength!"

Michelle giggled. "Sure, Momma Peach."

Momma Peach let go of Michelle. The hopeful future

was so bright that the looming arrival of Mr. Penlin had faded from her mind. "Now we gotta talk about baby names. Now, listen to me, there are some fine names out there, but I am very fond of Able and Michelle and—"

"If my child is a girl, her name is going to be Caroline Michelle. And if he's a boy," Michelle smiled gently, "he's going to be named after your husband and Able."

Momma Peach couldn't fight back her tears. "Well, now," she said and hurried back to the supper dishes before a dam broke loose, "that's mighty fine. Yes, sir and yes ma'am, that's mighty fine indeed. I am so honored."

Michelle picked up the dish rag and looked at Momma Peach. She loved her Momma Peach more than words could say. Momma Peach was her heart. She began to tell Momma Peach what kind of house she wanted to raise her family in when Able rushed into the kitchen, tripped over his feet, and crashed down to the floor. "Penlin just pulled up," Able said from the floor as he rolled his eyes at himself. "Darn shoelaces," he mumbled, "why can't you stay laced, huh?"

Michelle hurried over to Able and helped him stand up. "We'll worry about your clumsiness later, honey. Right now, we have a case to handle. Let's go, Momma Peach."

Momma Peach wiped her hands on the yellow apron she was wearing and walked out of the kitchen with Michelle. It was time to get back to business.

CHAPTER FIVE

*H*eath Penlin set down a black suitcase on the floor with an easy hand. "I'm running behind schedule, I'm afraid," he said in a businesslike tone.

Mitchel calmly slid the guest registry form across the front counter. "Go ahead and sign in, Mr. Smith," he said in a relaxed tone that even fooled Momma Peach. "Your room is waiting for you."

"I am tired," Heath lied. He glanced over his shoulder and saw Momma Peach standing beside the fireplace next to Sam. As far as he could tell, the two were talking about fishing. Michelle and Able were nowhere in sight.

"Want me to go and fetch your equipment?" Mitchel asked.

"My equipment?" Heath asked, returning his attention back to Mitchel. "Oh, yes, my camera. I have my camera in my suitcase," he recovered smoothly.

Mitchel knew Heath was lying but nodded his head as if he believed the man. "Well, Mr. Smith, I don't know much about photography. My wife, now she loved to take photos. She must have taken over a thousand photos before she went on to heaven and—"

"Yes, yes, I'm sure her photos are very nice," Heath cut Mitchel off and scribbled hurriedly to fill out the guest registry form. "Those two people standing over there, who are they?" he inquired, even though he knew.

"Oh, just a couple of guests up from Georgia," Mitchel explained. He took the guest registry form and examined it. "The room deposit is to be paid in cash, as we talked about on the phone. Your credit card will be charged for each night you stay. Breakfast is at seven, lunch at noon and supper at six. The kitchen is open for snacks and the front lobby is open all night." Mitchel placed the guest registry form into a brown folder. "Now listen to me, Mr. Smith, and listen closely. Stay on the marked trails and don't go wandering off. I had a man wander off a trail once and I didn't find his body until the snow melted."

Heath pulled a black wallet from the back pocket of the expensive gray slacks he was wearing. He fished out the required room deposit and handed the cash to Mitchel. "I understand. I'll stay on the marked trails."

96

Mitchel took the cash from Heath, handed him his room key, and pointed at the staircase. "One warning...we have a cranky guest staying with us. The man is down at the lake right now. He's been very rude to everyone, including me. I have a good mind to make him leave and I might just do so when he comes back from the lake. But in any case, you might be smart to steer clear of him."

"Sound advice," Heath said in a tight voice.

Momma Peach cast an eye at Heath and soaked in his appearance: short black hair and a sharp, handsome face. His green eyes were calculating and could not hide his cool disdain. Fancy gray suit. Yep, she thought, a criminal if she ever saw one—a clever criminal at that. "Well," she said in a tired voice, "it's getting time for me to go stare at the back of my eyelids."

"Yeah, me too," Sam agreed and let out a yawn. He looked at Mitchel. "Wake me up with the sun, okay Mitchel? I want to get in a full day's worth of fishing."

"Me too," Momma Peach added. "How about you," she said to Heath, "do you fish, mister?"

"No," Heath said and picked up his suitcase. "I don't fish."

"Too bad," Momma Peach said and let out a loud yawn. "My, what a day, what a day."

"That's our cue," Michelle whispered to Able from the

top of the stairs, where they listened from around the corner. Able nodded and followed Michelle around the corner and then down the staircase. "Are you still up, Momma Peach?" Michelle asked, surprised. "Able and I figured you would be asleep by now."

"Oh, you know me, baby. I can't lay down after a big meal. I decided to have some coffee with Mr. Sam and talk about our fishing trip tomorrow."

"I'm excited about our fishing trip," Michelle said and then looked at Heath. "A new guest, I see. I hope you're nicer than that jerk who went down to the lake."

"Yeah," Able added and then winced.

Heath studied the four people standing in the lobby. As far as he could tell, Marc had not let on who he was or what his mission at the lodge was. "I was warned about that guest," Heath told Michelle and began walking toward the staircase with his suitcase. "I'll be sure to steer clear of him."

"No sense in letting a rotten apple ruin the entire barrel," Momma Peach said in a pleasant voice. "Alaska is far too beautiful to let one worm spoil the whole bushel."

"You're right," Sam said and stretched his back. "Well, folks, I'm off to bed. Momma Peach, I'll walk you upstairs."

"We'll stay down next to the fire for a while," Michelle said and made a flirty face at Able. "Able and I want some...alone time."

"I see," Momma Peach said and winked at Able. "You behave yourself."

Able blushed. "Yes, Momma Peach."

Heath decided that his four victims were clueless as to who he and Marc were. He went up the staircase and made his way down the hallway toward his room, which was directly across from Marc's room. The door to Marc's room was slightly ajar, he noticed. Heath glanced over his shoulder, saw that the hallway was empty, and eased Marc's door open. And there, sitting on the floor, was a box of matches. Heath bent down, snatched up the box of matches, and hurried into his room.

"What have you been doing, Marc?" he muttered to himself as he kicked the room door shut with his foot and dropped his suitcase down onto the floor. With careful eyes, he studied the matchbox. There was something wrong. He eased it open. "The key," he hissed. The key was missing.

Heath shoved the matchbox down into the front right pocket of his expensive gray suit and walked over to the bed. He sat down on the red and blue quilt and rubbed his hand over his mouth as he stared out at the dark space above the trees. "What did you do with the key, Marc... or...maybe you don't have the key?" Heath looked to his left, toward the room door. "Maybe that woman has it?"

As Heath pondered on certain possibilities, Momma Peach walked to her room with Sam. Sam entered Momma Peach's room with her and eased the door closed. "He's found the matchbox by now," he said in a quiet tone.

"He sure has," Momma Peach agreed. She moved to the window in her room and pulled back the curtain. "Now we wait and see if that snake comes back from the lake." Momma Peach peered into the dark night. She had never seen such a dark night in all her life. The dark seemed to float down from the sky while floating up from the ground at the same time and settle over every living thing like a black mist. Yet, she thought, the darkness was not scary—just so vast it was lonely.

Sam sat down in the armchair and crossed his right leg over his left knee. "And then what?" he asked. "Do we wait and see what those two killers might do?" Sam shook his head, not liking the idea.

"All we can do is wait," Momma Peach told Sam in a calm but worried voice. "Michelle is downstairs. She's going to watch the snake when he comes back from the lake. You're carrying a gun. Mr. Mitchel is carrying a gun. Michelle is carrying a gun. Able, bless his heart, well, he's better off with a broom stick and I have my pocketbook. Until high noon, baby, all we can do is wait for the outlaw to draw first."

"Poetic," Sam told Momma Peach. He yawned. "This old man is sleepy," he pointed out. "I hope we're not in for a long night."

"I worry that we are," Momma Peach told Sam and yawned herself. "Oh, them there yawns are the most contagious critters in the world."

"Tell me about it," Sam agreed, yawning yet again.

Momma Peach turned away from the window. "By now, that man is realizing that silver key you found is missing. He's wondering if I have the key or if his sidekick Marc has the key. He's probably also wondering what the matchbox was doing on the floor. Was the matchbox dropped or left there deliberately? But because the door was open, courtesy of Mr. Mitchel, he's most likely leaning toward the idea that the matchbox might have been dropped. Now, I can't read minds, baby, but this is what my own mind is thinking."

"So you're trying to play one snake against another. I get that, Momma Peach," Sam said.

Momma Peach nodded her head. "Mr. Sam, that man down there at the lake, when he was in the lobby with us I looked into his eyes...he didn't have a soul. Mr. Penlin is a paycheck to him and nothing else. I want to make Mr. Penlin start wondering just how trustworthy his hired snake is."

"But that still doesn't change the fact that Penlin came here to possibly kill us," Sam pointed out.

"Maybe Penlin came here to kill his hired thug," Momma Peach pointed out. "If I can make Mr. Penlin believe that a certain four little mice are blind after all, and that his little snake is playing a game, then maybe he'll kill the snake and go away and leave us alone."

"That's kinda thin," Sam pointed out.

"Don't I know it, baby," Momma Peach fretted. "All we can do is wait and see what card Mr. Penlin and the snake outside lay down."

"It's going to be a long night," Sam said in a tired voice.

Momma Peach walked over to the bed and sat down. "I hate not knowing if the trap I set will fool the rat."

"Well," Sam said, "I think we convinced Penlin that we were in the dark about what's going on and who he is. Penlin didn't seem too worried when he walked upstairs. So if he did find the box of matches, he could lean toward suspecting that his arsonist and thug is possibly playing a more dangerous game."

"And maybe," Momma Peach reiterated in a hopeful voice, "leave without causing trouble."

"You don't believe that."

"No," Momma Peach said in a miserable voice. "The snake outside, Mr. Sam, isn't going to leave here until he hurts someone. I'm just hoping Mr. Penlin will kill his own snake before he strikes us. It seems to me that Mr. Penlin wants the least amount of light cast on him as possible. We have that working in our favor."

"An ex-con working to sabotage a cruise ship to gather the insurance money wouldn't want a lot of light on his face," Sam agreed. "So, we'll sit here and wait and see what happens." Sam reached under his shirt and pulled out the gun Mitchel had given him. "I sure hope I don't have to use this."

"I sure hope you don't either, baby," Momma Peach told Sam and resisted the urge to lay down on the bed and fall asleep. The waiting game was now on.

Out in the darkness, the body of Marc Stravinsky was floating face-down in the lake. The man was dead. His killer was on the loose, moving soundlessly through the forest. But the killer was not Heath Penlin. Heath Penlin had arrived alone to kill Marc without leaving a trace of evidence. He didn't see any point in killing Momma Peach or her friends. At least, not yet. His intentions were to kill Marc and see if the man's death ended his problems. If not, then he was prepared to take more dramatic measures. He would clean up these loose ends by any means necessary.

"Let's hope it doesn't come to that," Heath said and rested his eyes on the black suitcase sitting at his feet.

Mitchel yawned. His body felt exhausted, but as usual, his mind wouldn't shut down and go to sleep. So as usual, he wandered out into the lobby and knelt down by the fireplace until he managed to get a warm fire going and a pot of coffee brewing. "Four in the morning, right on time," he said, tossing a log onto the fire and standing up. The fire crackled and began to warm him. "Guess I won't be able to sleep well until I join my wife in heaven."

Outside, a strong wind pushed up against the lodge. Winter was coming early. Mitchel listened to the wind and thought back through time and found precious memories of his wife. He saw his wife standing down by the lake, caught up in working on one of her paintings. There she stood, sweet, lovely, and beautiful under a soft winter sky, painting a white wonderland. Mitchel felt tears sting the corners of his eyes. "None of that," he spoke softly and tucked the green flannel shirt he was wearing down into a pair of brown pants. "No tears," he pleaded and hurried to return his focus to the fire.

After drinking a cup of coffee and eating a bran muffin, Mitchel decided to take a walk down to the lake. The moon was dark and the land was silent and asleep. The lake was always peaceful in the early hours of the morning, resting and full of dreams. Mitchel enjoyed taking walks down to the lake and standing out on the wooden dock. He liked listening to the lake sleep, the land rest, and the sky dream. "Let's go get some fresh air."

Mitchel refilled his coffee mug and left the lodge. Outside he headed down toward the lake, taking a well-groomed trail that was easy to follow in the dark. Mitchel knew the trail by heart and never took a flashlight with him during his early morning walks down to the lake; all he needed was a cup of coffee and his rifle, just in case he bumped into a bear looking for an early morning snack. Mitchel didn't expect to see any bears as he walked down the trail, surrounded by dark trees swaying back and forth in a strong wind.

The further he walked down the trail, the more he realized the wind was whispering through the trees in a strange way. Mitchel realized he had never before heard the birds so silent in the pre-dawn hours. It was as if...the silence was somehow warning Mitchel that something was amiss. Mitchel felt the hairs stand up on the back of his neck, paused, glanced down at the lake and debated whether to listen to his gut and turn back or push forward. "Come on, old man, push forward. Just like the old days when you were a soldier in the Army. Just a blustery day." The wind whined. Mitchel gripped his mug of coffee, took a drink, and continued to walk down to the lake.

In the trees at the water's edge, a pair of eyes tracked him silently, watching his every step with deadly calm. There was not a single sound to warn Mitchel, who strode on confidently.

When Mitchel reached the lake, he walked out onto the wooden dock and stared out at the dark water. The lake was large and shaped like a smooth-edged skipping stone. Some parts of the lake went down as far as fifty feet while other areas were merely two feet deep. Years back, a married couple had decided to put on some fancy scuba diving gear and explore the lake. To Mitchel's surprise, the couple mapped out the entire lake and presented him with a copy of the map before they left. He had been most intrigued to see that it showed a steep underwater drop-off, a mere twenty feet out from the wooden dock. Mitchel didn't like deep water but had never felt threatened by the immense depths of the lake. That moment in the darkness, as he stood staring out across the lake, the depths seemed to reach up for him with watery fingers that sent a horrible chill into his heart. "Easy now," Mitchel said, taking a step back. He slung the coffee out of his mug and yanked his rifle off his shoulder. "Easy, old man. Don't get spooked."

Mitchel slowly turned around and searched the darkness with his eyes. The winds were whining at him, and the birdsong was still silent, and that silence was like a siren begging him to run. Someone or something was in the darkness watching him. Mitchel felt a pair of eyes locked on his every movement. Was it merely a wolf or a moose? Or was it something more troubling?

The lodge stood off in the far distance with only the light from the lobby windows giving off any sign of life. "Who is out there?" Mitchel yelled through the crying winds, letting his eyes examine the darkness. He knew the land. He knew the trees. He knew the lake—but darkness was impartial and hid the good and the bad from sight.

Mitchel brought his rifle up and aimed into the darkness. As he did, he felt something bump into the wooden dock. Startled, he spun around and fired at the lake, and the shot echoed against the water and the surrounding hills.

The sound of a rifle woke Sam up from a shallow sleep. He jumped out of the chair in Momma Peach's room, ran to the window, and looked out into the early morning. "Momma Peach," he said.

"I heard, baby," Momma Peach said, crawling out of her bed. She hurried over to the door and yanked it open. "I'm going to check on the others."

Momma Peach ran out into the hallway just as Michelle raced out of her room, throwing her black leather jacket over a dark gray dress. "You heard the gunshot?" she asked Momma Peach.

"I heard."

The door to Able's room opened. Able came hopping out, trying to tie his shoe. He lost his balance and crashed down onto the hallway floor. "I heard a gunshot," he said, ignoring his clumsiness.

Sam stepped out into the hallway and closed the door to Momma Peach's room. He lifted his shirt and pulled out the gun Mitchel had given him. "Momma Peach, you and Able stay in the lobby. Michelle and I will go outside and take a look around."

Momma Peach agreed and accompanied Able down into the lobby. She spotted a warm fire dancing in the fireplace and a fresh pot of coffee resting over the fire. "Mr. Mitchel must be up. Me and Able will go check his apartment."

"Good," Sam said and looked at Michelle. "Stay at my side."

"You can count on it," Michelle promised and walked over to the lobby door. "The door is unlocked. Sam, we better hurry."

Sam looked at Momma Peach. "Check Mitchel's apartment, and stay together," he pleaded.

Momma Peach got her short legs moving, ran behind the front counter and located a green metal flashlight. She handed the flashlight to Sam. "I will be glue and Able will be paper," she promised Sam.

Sam nodded his head and hurried out the front door with Michelle.

Michelle walked outside into a powerful wind that began grabbing at her long, black hair. "The gunshot came from the lake, I think," she told Sam, climbing down the front porch steps.

"Agreed," Sam said, casting his eyes around in the darkness. He had never seen a darkness so thick and consuming in all of his life. What a night for the moon to be asleep. "Stay close," he told Michelle and debated on whether to turn on the flashlight or not. The light from the flashlight would make him and Michelle a clear and easy target. "Can you see okay?"

"Enough," Michelle said, reading Sam's worry. She bent down and took out her gun from the ankle holster. "Let's move." They set off down the trail to the lake.

On the dock, Mitchel tried to steel his nerves and calm his racing pulse after firing the rifle. Something was bumping into the dock, driven by the fierce wind and the rippling waves on the surface of the lake. Whatever the something was, it wasn't a mere broken tree limb. He could hear it making a sickeningly soft, sodden noise every time it hit the dock. Mitchel aimed his rifle down at the lake surface and moved forward carefully and slowly. When he reached the edge, he looked down at the dark water and saw a shadow floating in the water, face down. His blood went cold but he managed to stay calm. He lowered the barrel of the rifle and touched the back of the shadow. The shadow was a human being. "Oh boy," Mitchel said. He spun around and searched the darkness again. Someone was coming down the trail toward the lake. Mitchel dropped down onto one knee and aimed into the darkness. "Who's there?" he yelled out in a fierce voice.

"Sam and Michelle," Sam called out.

Mitchel saw a light appear on the trail. A minute later, Sam and Michelle appeared. Mitchel felt relief course through his veins. He raced off the wooden dock and greeted his friends with a grateful voice. "I'm glad it was you two and not anyone else." Mitchel tossed a thumb over his shoulder. "There's a dead body in the lake."

"Sam, let me have the flashlight," Michelle said. Sam handed Michelle the flashlight and followed her out onto the wooden dock. Michelle walked to the end of the dock and aimed the flashlight down at the dark water. She spotted Marc floating face down, in the same clothes he had been wearing before. "Here," she told Sam and handed him the flashlight, shoved her gun back into the ankle holster she was wearing, reached down into the lake, and grabbed the back of Marc's shirt and began pulling him out of the lake. Sam quickly handed Mitchel the flashlight and helped Michelle heave the body out of the lake and up onto the dock. "Flashlight," Michelle told

Mitchel, catching her breath. Mitchel handed Michelle the flashlight. "I need to examine the body. Sam, turn him over. I need to check for bullet or stab wounds."

"Sure thing," Sam said and flipped Marc's body over.

Michelle eased forward on her knees and examined Marc's face. "He's been dead for a while," she pointed out and continued examining the body. The examination stopped at the throat. "This man has been strangled to death," she said and pointed to Marc's neck. "See the red line going around his neck?"

Sam and Mitchel leaned closer to the body and spotted the livid red mark Michelle was pointing at. "Looks like maybe...fishing line?" Sam suggested.

Michelle bit down on her lower lip. "This guy wouldn't have gone down without a fight." Michelle looked up at Sam. "Heath Penlin didn't appear to have been in any altercation when he arrived," she pointed out.

"Yeah," Sam agreed. "The man's suit was neatly pressed and his hair was in perfect order. Are you thinking Penlin has someone else with him?"

"I heard Mr. Penlin drive up in the brown Jeep Wrangler he's driving," Mitchel told Sam. "I watched him get out of the jeep from the front window of my apartment. He arrived alone." Mitchel stood up and backed away from Marc's body. He scanned the darkness beyond the line of trees. That eerie silence continued. "Someone is out there in the darkness watching us," he said in a low, worried tone.

Michelle retrieved her gun and stood up. She searched the darkness with her eyes. "Mitchel, you fired the gunshot we heard, didn't you?"

"I did," Mitchel replied. "I guess my nerves are tight...when I felt something hit the dock I turned and fired into the dark."

Sam leaned forward and let the darkness into his eyes. Someone was standing out in the darkness watching them. When he lived in the desert he learned how to sense the presence of a rattlesnake before he saw the snake. There was a rattlesnake hiding in the darkness, coiled up and prepared to strike again.

Only this snake didn't have a rattle—this snake was silent and had already melted away into the darkness beyond the tree line, cutting up the hillside toward the lodge. And then, the snake unsheathed a wickedly sharp knife from his belt, cut the phone lines at the side of the building, slashed every tire on every vehicle in the darkness, and vanished without a trace back into the concealing thicket of the forest.

Dawn had not even broken, but the lodge had been crippled by a killer.

Inside the lodge, Momma Peach walked Able back into the lobby and found Heath Penlin standing beside the fireplace dressed in his fancy suit. "I heard a gunshot," he said in a tone that tried to sound calm but was nevertheless tainted with concern.

Momma Peach stared at Heath. The man had his right hand hidden in the front pocket of his jacket which meant he was hiding a gun. "We heard a gunshot, too," she said in an upset tone that should have won an award. "Mr. Mitchel is missing. He didn't come back from his morning walk. Oh, my," Momma Peach grabbed Able's hand. "I hope no bear got him."

Able quickly caught on. "I'm sure Mr. Mitchel is okay...I hope."

Heath looked at the front door. Marc was missing, too. He checked the man's room before coming downstairs and found it empty. All he could do for the moment was wait.

Momma Peach wasn't in the mood to wait. She walked behind the front desk, ready to play her part, set on calling the local sheriff to report the lodge owner as a missing person. But her hopes were dashed when she found the phone dead. "Phone line is out," she told Able in a worried voice and put the phone down.

"What?" Heath asked. He ran over to the front counter

and tried the phone. "Dead," he said and nearly slammed the phone down.

"Yes sir," Momma Peach said and walked over to Able and took his hand. "Baby, maybe we better do a head count and go upstairs and wake up that rude man. I think it's better if all the guests gather in the lobby."

Heath didn't want to chance anyone entering Marc's room. "I'll go upstairs and knock on his door," he offered. "I need to get something from my room anyway."

Momma Peach watched Heath walk upstairs, worry plainly clear in his tense posture. "Interesting how that man knows what room to go to," she commented to Able in an undertone. "He's awful nervous, and when a criminal gets nervous, they don't think clearly and make mistakes."

Able stared up at the staircase. He watched Heath vanish. "Momma Peach," he whispered in a worried voice, "the phone is out. Someone must have cut the phone lines. We need to get Michelle, Sam, and Mitchel and try and make it to the sheriff's office."

"I'm inclined to agree with you, baby," Momma Peach patted Able's hand. "It's clear Mr. Penlin didn't cut the phone line and—"

The door to the lobby opened just then. Mitchel appeared and walked into the lobby. Michelle and Sam brought up the rear. Michelle looked at Momma Peach. "We found a dead body in the lake."

"The snake?" Momma Peach asked.

"Yes," Sam said. He closed the front door and locked it. "Appears the man was strangled to death."

"I need to call the sheriff," Mitchel said. He handed Sam his rifle and hurried over to the front counter.

"Phone is dead," Momma Peach told Mitchel.

Mitchel stopped in his tracks. He looked at Michelle and Sam. Michelle walked over to Able and took his hand reassuringly. "Well then, we'll drive to town."

"Someone slashed the tires on every vehicle outside," Michelle said, her voice hard.

Sam walked over to the fireplace and stared into the fire. "Whoever the killer is, he...or she...wants to trap us in the lodge."

Able looked into Michelle's eyes. "Mr. Penlin came downstairs. He looked worried and didn't know that the phone lines had been cut. He went back upstairs to see if the man you found dead is in his room."

Michelle's eyes darted to the staircase. Seconds later, Heath came walking down the stairs. He spotted everyone standing in the lobby with uneasy expressions on their faces. Something was horribly wrong, which meant it was time for him to exit stage right. He would deal later with Marc, who was still missing. "I think I'm going to check out and leave," he told Mitchel in a smooth tone of voice.

"You can't leave," Mitchel told Heath.

"Why not?" Heath demanded.

"Because someone slashed the tires on every vehicle parked outside," Mitchel fired back. "On top of that, the phone is out, and to make matters much worse, we found a dead body in the lake."

"The body belongs to the man you went to check on," Momma Peach told Heath.

"What?" Heath asked, shocked. His mind raced. Who would kill Marc? Who could kill Marc, was a better question. Marc was a trained killer. "How?"

"Strangled to death," Michelle informed Heath. She nodded at his right hand. "If you have a gun in your pocket, please take it out, sir. My name is Detective Michelle Chan and as of now, I'm in charge of this crime scene."

Heath hesitated and then slowly pulled out an ugly black gun from his right pocket. "I heard a gunshot. I got nervous, okay?" he defended himself.

"It's illegal to carry a gun into Alaska without declaring it," Mitchel pointed out.

Michelle quickly capitalized on the situation. "Sir, I'm going to need your gun. There are laws against carrying guns across state lines."

Heath locked his eyes on the gun Michelle was holding in her hand. As it stood, the odds were against him—for now. He had a second gun hidden upstairs in his room. "It's dangerous for a photographer to go traipsing about the woods unarmed," he told Michelle and handed her his gun. "No government has a right to place my life in danger," he finished, attempting to come across as a freedom fighter.

"Laws are laws," Michelle replied. Deep down, though, she would never admit it to a criminal, she agreed that gun laws were restrictive, and everyone should have the freedom to defend their lives. However, she was taking a gun away from a criminal and that's what mattered at the moment. Lawful people deserved freedom—criminals deserved bars. "Okay," she said and looked at Momma Peach, "we have a killer on the loose and as it stands, we're stranded."

Momma Peach bit down on her lower lip. She studied Heath's eyes. The man didn't kill his hired snake. No, sir and no ma'am. There was a different killer on the prowl and even Mr. Heath Penlin was mighty scared. Momma Peach had to admit that she was mighty scared, too.

From the depths of the wooded hills, as dawn broke, the killer stared down at the isolated lodge in satisfaction. Thunder clouds began to gather over the landscape, filling with the dark gray promise of a heavy rain. "When night falls," the poisonous voice hissed. "When night falls, I'll be back."

CHAPTER SIX

*M*omma Peach wasn't sure if she wanted to confront Heath about his true identity or not. With Marc dead, her plan to try and play snake against snake was no longer needed. As a matter of fact, Momma Peach thought, chewing on a bite of scrambled eggs, it appeared that Mr. Heath Penlin came to Alaska alone, which meant that unless the man intended to commit a monumental act of multiple homicide, he had most likely no ill intentions toward anyone except his hired killer. Momma Peach was certain Heath had traveled to the lodge to kill Marc and then leave without hurting anyone else—or so it seemed to her; criminals were a mighty funny breed who could easily change their stripes in a matter of seconds. But as it stood, Momma Peach felt confident that her theory was on track. The matchbox and the silver key were of no more importance, since there was a different killer to worry about. Besides, Marc was dead, leaving only the head cobra to deal with, and the head cobra wasn't as much of a threat as she had assumed he would be. The man seemed focused on money, not murder.

"Were you expecting rain today?" Momma Peach asked Mitchel instead of speaking her thoughts.

Mitchel leaned back on his wooden chair and glanced at the window in the small dining room where he, Momma Peach, Sam, Michelle and Able were eating breakfast. Heath was upstairs in his room. "Wind brought in the rain," he told Momma Peach.

Momma Peach dipped her fork to cut a warm flapjack and picked up a piece. Except for a killer being on the loose, the morning was quiet and cozy. The dining room, although somewhat small, was rustic and inviting. Like the rest of the lodge, the walls were made of smoothed logs and the hardwood floor shone with polish. The curtains hanging over the window framed a beautiful view down to the crystal clear lake. The dining room table was long enough to seat twenty guests and well-worn by time—a dining room fit for the true wilderness around it. It was a far cry from the mundane dining rooms to be found at most motels littered across the American landscape.

Momma Peach gazed out at the rain. "It rained in the desert, it rained in Georgia, it rained in Seattle and now it's raining in Alaska. Oh, I am going to become so waterlogged my skin will never smooth out. Give me strength, give me strength."

"I like the rain," Able confessed. "It's kinda...cozy sitting here listening to the rain fall outside."

"Oh, I love the rain, too, baby. I just like to fuss," Momma Peach tipped Able a wink. "And yes, baby, it's very cozy sitting in this dining room eating breakfast with the people I love."

Able gave Momma Peach a loving look. Momma Peach was taking over his heart. "Breakfast is delicious. I've never had flapjacks this good before."

"A dash of Momma Peach is always good for the stomach," Momma Peach beamed. She looked at Michelle, who was sitting across from her and frowned. "What's on your mind, honey?" she asked, reading the worried look in Michelle's eyes.

Michelle picked at her breakfast and then set down the fork in her hand. She looked around the dining room table at everyone and focused back on Momma Peach. "Momma Peach, the man I fought with upstairs was pretty strong. Whoever killed him...strangled him...couldn't have been a weakling. Also," Michelle pointed out. "I'm trying to understand how a man like that could be surprised. The killer must have snuck up on him in the dark, otherwise there would have been a fight. When Sam and I went back down to the lake and carried the body up to Mitchel's utility shed, I reexamined the body more carefully. I didn't find any signs on the body that pointed to a struggle. No bruises, no marks, no ripped clothing, nothing."

"I think what Michelle is trying to imply," Sam cut in and took a sip of hot coffee, "is that our killer has some serious wilderness skills."

"I felt the killer watching me from the lake," Mitchel said and shook off a chill. His face became dark with dread. "Unless you know this land the way I do, you can't possibly maneuver around in the dark without getting lost. Also, if you're not walking on a marked trail, if you're out walking in the brush, well, I would be able to hear anyone walking in the brush and I didn't hear a sound."

Momma Peach chewed on her flapjack. The case of the doomed cruise ship had turned into the case of the invisible wilderness killer. Dealing with one dangerous case was enough—dealing with two was overwhelming. "Mr. Mitchel, forgive me for asking this, but do you have any enemies? Folks who might want to do you harm, as sweet as you are, bless your heart."

Mitchel shook his head no. "Not a soul," he said truthfully. "I'm an easy-going sort of man who gets along with most people. About the only trouble I ever had was with the family of the man who wandered off the trail and died. The fella whose body I found when the snow melted."

"What kind of trouble?" Michelle inquired.

"Oh, legal trouble mostly," Mitchel continued. He took a sip of hot coffee and looked back out the dining room window. "The man's wife tried to sue me. Her lawsuit fell flat, though, because the trails actually cut through publicly-owned land and so the liability was ultimately the state's. The man's son, a fussy young guss, threatened my lodge but nothing ever came of it. That was, oh...five years back. I haven't heard a word from those people since."

"The man who died, who was he?" Michelle asked. Momma Peach perked up her ears.

"A doctor from Los Angeles," Mitchel told Michelle. "A man named Bert Dennerton. I believe the man was a surgeon, if I remember correctly. He came to my lodge on a hunting trip with two other men...I can't remember the names, though. My memory isn't what it used to be, I'm afraid."

"You're doing just fine, baby," Momma Peach assured Mitchel. "You keep on talking and don't worry what your memory might forget."

Mitchel gave Momma Peach an appreciative look. "Thank you," he said and took another sip of coffee and continued. "The three men went out hunting. I warned them to stay on the hunting trails before they left, same as I warned you folks when you arrived. Sometime later, two of the men returned without Dr. Dennerton. It was getting dark by the time the two men returned to the lodge and a hard snow was beginning to fall." Mitchel shook his head. "I asked what hunting trail the two men had taken...they took the Deep North trail, which most hunters like to take. The trail was already cut into the land when I bought the lodge. I keep the trail maintained because it's good for hunting. At the end of the trail, I have a large wooden sign nailed to a tree that reads 'Stay Within The Marked Area'."

"Marked area?" Momma Peach asked. She wasn't familiar with hunting.

"I tied bright orange ribbons around trees at the end of the trail, forming a wide circle, giving a hunter room to spread out off the trail. I even put up a couple of hunting stands back there. I believe in good hunting, but I also believe in safety first. This land can swallow a man up whole if he's not careful. The orange ribbons show a hunter how far he can go out without losing his way."

"I'm guessing Mr. Mitchel didn't find Dr. Dennerton inside the marked area," Momma Peach stated.

"No, Momma Peach, I sure didn't," Mitchel shook his head with sadness. "The search parties had no luck all that winter and finally gave it up when the snows got too deep. When spring came, I grabbed a bag full of orange ribbons, walked to the end of the Deep North trail same as every year, and began working my way into the land, tying a ribbon to a tree every few feet along the way to make sure I didn't get lost myself. But I made the circle a bit bigger that year, because I had been planning to expand it for a while. I found Dr. Dennerton's body under a tree...it wasn't a pretty sight. The man had... wandered four miles north of the marked area. Took me all day to get his body back to the lodge. My poor wife was about ready to call in the Army to go and search for me by the time I came off the trail. But...calling the man's family was even harder."

"What about Dr. Dennerton's two friends, baby?" Momma Peach asked.

Mitchel shrugged his shoulders. "After the search team that was organized failed to find Dr. Dennerton, the two men left. What else could they do?" Mitchel shook his head again. "If only..."

"If only what?" Michelle asked.

"Well," Mitchel said and let out a deep breath, "the two men hunting with Dr. Dennerton claimed they last saw him moving east. So, that's where the search team looked. If only we had searched north. But you have to understand that this is Alaska and the search team consisted mainly of volunteers...besides the sheriff and me, there was maybe twenty of us at the most. And to make matters worse, we went out looking for a missing man in a fierce snowstorm. But still, if only we had looked north and not east...it was a lost cause."

"Maybe Dr. Dennerton's friends didn't want you searching north?" Michelle suggested. "Maybe you were deliberately pointed in the wrong direction?"

Mitchel shook his head no. "No, Dr. Dennerton's two friends...those two men...they had no harm in them. I could tell. They were worried about Dr. Dennerton and didn't leave my lodge until the search was called off by the sheriff. I think they did spot Dr. Dennerton moving east but the man got lost and ended up traveling north."

Michelle trusted Mitchel's judgment. If Mitchel stated that Dr. Dennerton's two friends had no malice in them, she believed him. "Okay, so we focus back on the wife and son," she said. "You said Dr. Dennerton's son threatened your lodge. How?"

"With fire," Mitchel answered Michelle. "The boy was upset and placed all blame and responsibility squarely on my lap. As I said, he was a fussy little guss, but harmless. All bark, no bite. You know how some eighteen-year-old boys are. They have to act tough in order to hide their pain."

"Eighteen...that would make Dr. Dennerton's son twenty-three," Able pointed out. "That's plenty enough time for someone to join the military and get some training under his belt."

Michelle looked at Able. "Military?" she asked.

Able looked back at Michelle. Michelle wasn't giving him

a look of disapproval. Instead, her eyes hungered for him to continue with his thought. "I was just thinking that if Dr. Dennerton's son wanted revenge, maybe he committed himself to some form of training. You said that the man you found dead didn't show any signs of a struggle, right?"

"Right," Michelle said.

"And Sam said the killer has wilderness skills, right, Sam?"

"Most likely," Sam agreed.

"And Mitchel said Dr. Dennerton was a city doctor, which meant his son was a city person, too," Able continued. Momma Peach beamed. Able was jumping on board with both feet. "Dr. Dennerton's son threatened Mitchel's lodge with fire but never carried out the threat. But what if he decided to wait?"

"That's my boy," Momma Peach told Able. "Oh, let your mind speak, let it speak."

Able blushed. "I was just...kinda thinking...that's all."

Michelle squeezed Able's hand. "That's what good detectives do, honey," she smiled.

"No, wait a minute, hold on," Mitchel objected, "you two are way out in left field. Dr. Dennerton's son isn't the killer. That boy was all smoke and no fire. Besides," Mitchel said in a pleading tone, "why would that boy wait five years? I'm sure he's just finished college by now."

Momma Peach understood Mitchel's objection. "Can you tell us any more about Dr. Dennerton, his wife or his son, Mr. Mitchel?" she asked, hoping Mitchel's mind would dredge up any lost facts.

Mitchel rubbed his chin. "Well," he said, "all I remember about Dr. Dennerton's wife and son is that they arrived at my lodge one day out of the blue and threatened me with a lawsuit. Before they left, Dr. Dennerton's son threatened to burn down my lodge. I ran him out with my rifle. I never heard a word from either one of them since. My lawyer handled the lawsuit for me and in the end when the smoke cleared, the lawsuit fell flat. I didn't even have to step foot in a courtroom."

"I see," Momma Peach said as her mind latched onto a thought. "Mr. Mitchel, when Dr. Dennerton's son threatened to burn down your lovely lodge here, did you return his threat with one of your own? Now don't get mad at me for asking such a question, but sometimes," Momma Peach eased forward on eggshells, "tempers do run loose in the heat of the moment."

Mitchel considered Momma Peach's question. He took a sip of coffee and thought back in time. "I was standing next to the fireplace...it was snowing outside...my wife was asking Dr. Dennerton's wife to leave our lodge..." Mitchel closed his eyes. He saw a tall, ugly, black-haired boy staring at him with sour eyes. "I told the boy to leave...he pointed to the fireplace and told me he was going to burn my lodge down...I had my rifle leaning against the fireplace...I grabbed it and told him if he ever tried...and then...oh my goodness." Mitchel popped his eyes open. "Oh, dear goodness."

"What is it?" Sam asked.

"I..." Mitchel looked at Momma Peach with shameful eyes. "I did. I threatened to kill that boy...I told him I would fill him full of holes if he ever stepped foot on my land again..." Mitchel bowed his head. "Oh, how could I?"

"Don't be so hard on yourself," Able tried to comfort Mitchel.

Mitchel kept his head low. "My wife...the cancer was so tough on her that year...I wanted Dr. Dennerton's wife and son out of my lodge..." Mitchel felt his memory of the day he threatened to shoot Dr. Dennerton's son forced into exact, clear detail. "When Dr. Dennerton's son threatened to burn down my cabin I saw my wife's face bundled up in fear. I exploded...and even worse...I struck Dr. Dennerton's son with my rifle and knocked the boy to the ground...and then I...fired a shot into the floor...after that, I chased them out into the snow. But," Mitchel raised his eyes, "it was just a moment of weakness. How could it be? How can that create a killer?" he begged.

"It didn't, Mr. Mitchel. And we're not saying that Dr. Dennerton's son is the killer," Momma Peach told Mitchel in a soothing voice. "We're trying to create a list of suspects, that's all. You begin a list with possible enemies and work your way down. Now, is there anyone else besides Dr. Dennerton's wife and son who has caused you trouble?"

Mitchel shook his head. "Not a soul. I mean, besides a complaint here and there about the food or hot water running out. Dr. Dennerton was the worst. Poor man..."

Momma Peach saw sorrow sweep through Mitchel's eyes. The man was truly sorry about the death of a man who wandered away from the safe zone he had created for hunters. "Baby," Momma Peach spoke softly, "you didn't kill Dr. Dennerton. You can't blame yourself for the actions of another man. Dr. Dennerton didn't heed your warnings about the trail in foul weather, and that was his fault, not yours." She patted the back of his hand comfortingly and he nodded.

In the silence that followed, Michelle returned to her breakfast. As dangerous as this vacation had turned out to be, Mama Peach's flapjacks were out of this world, as always. As she took another delectable bite, she saw that Sam's eyes were thoughtful. "What are you thinking, Sam?"

"We're really reaching into thin air here," Sam told Michelle. "Sure, Dr. Dennerton's son threatened

Mitchel, but to say he's the killer? We need evidence, not speculation."

"I know that," Michelle agreed.

"Could it be that the dead man you dragged out of the lake had a sidekick that turned on him?" Able asked. Somehow his suggestion didn't fit well when he said it, and he shook his head uncertainly.

"Could be," Sam replied. He looked at Momma Peach. "Momma Peach?"

"No, sir and no ma'am," Momma Peach said in a firm voice, "I looked into that snake's eyes. He worked solo, baby. Yes, you better believe me when I tell you, I saw the truth. That snake slithered around alone."

Sam picked up his coffee mug and took a sip of coffee. "I trust you, Momma Peach."

Momma Peach raised her right finger and pointed up at the ceiling. "Mr. Heath Penlin isn't involved in the killing, either. I believe that man came here to kill his hired man, but now that he's already dead, he's done. He said he wanted to leave, after all. His criminal mind is racing around in a locked cell trying to find a way out."

"Which leaves us with the unknown again," Sam said.

"Which leaves us with a possible suspect," Michelle pointed out. "If I had a phone I could make a few calls and find out some facts about Dr. Dennerton's son."

"Nearest phone is two hours south," Mitchel told Michelle.

"Well," Sam said and finished off his coffee, "we can't sit here like sitting ducks and wait to be killed, one by one."

"We can't walk out of here, either," Mitchel warned Sam. "If we get caught out after dark...I don't want to end up strangled to death."

"I agree with Mitchel," Michelle told Sam. "If we try and walk to the nearest town we'll end up dead. Maybe that's what the killer wants us to try, actually. If we stay in the lodge we have a better chance of surviving."

"Surviving won't be enough, baby," Momma Peach joined in. "I know that a trap has to be set for the killer. I ain't gonna sit in this lodge and turn gray. We need a plan of action. Oh, give me strength, give me strength, if it ain't Old Joe driving me crazy it's someone just as loony in the head."

Momma Peach stopped talking when she heard footsteps approaching. Heath appeared in the doorway to the dining room. "I think I'll have some breakfast," he said and sat down a few chairs away from Mitchel. His face was a mask of frustration. "Any progress on the phone?"

"No," Mitchel said and handed Heath a brown plate. "Phone line was severed in four different places."

Heath shook his head and began dishing out scrambled

eggs onto his plate. "Don't you have any other way to get in touch with the sheriff?"

"No," Mitchel told Heath. "Never had any reason to need anything other than my telephone."

Heath fished a flapjack onto his plate and began eating. "Any idea who the killer is?" he asked Michelle. "You are a detective, right? You must have a lead or two by now."

Michelle remained patient. She had to manage Heath with caution. The man's threat level was a zero at the moment—but that could change at any moment. "No leads as of yet," she said in a professional tone.

Heath chewed on a bite of flapjack and glanced around the table at the people sitting before him. At least with the phone out, Michelle couldn't call and make any inquiries. But that also meant the unknown killer had free rein over the situation, as well. Heath felt frustrated, angry and confused. Who killed Marc? Why? Was the killer coming after him next? Was Marc connected to people he was unaware of? People who would want him dead, too? Heath didn't know. The questions buzzing around in his mind were driving him insane. He wanted answers. For the moment, however, he was trapped inside the lodge like an animal. "Do you have a plan, detective?" he finally asked.

"Wait," Michelle answered Heath.

"Wait?" Heath asked, forcing his voice to remain civil.

He was a business man, after all, and losing his cool wouldn't help him or the situation.

"What else can I do?" Michelle asked. "There is a killer prowling around outside. It's obvious to me the killer is very familiar with this land and this lodge. I'm not. I'm at a disadvantage, and so is everyone sitting here, except for Mitchel. If you want to go outside and search for the killer in this rain with your...cameras, then feel free."

Heath shook his head. "There's power in numbers," he said blandly and forked a bite of eggs into his mouth.

Momma Peach studied Heath. She wanted to slap the man bowlegged but decided to remain nonviolent for the time being. Instead, she attacked with her mind. "There sure is power in numbers, Mr. Penlin."

Heath's face went pale. He stopped chewing his food and looked at Momma Peach. "What...what did you call me?"

Michelle stepped up to the plate. "We know who you really are, Mr. Penlin. We knew before you arrived. We know you're connected to the man who was murdered, too. However, we don't believe you killed him, even though your intentions were to do so."

Momma Peach reached under the linen napkin beside her plate and fished out a silver key. "The snake you hired to set fire to one of the kitchens on the North Queen, Marc? He slipped a matchbox into the pocket of my rain jacket. I found the matchbox when I arrived here at the lodge. It had this key in it. Written inside the matchbox was a phone number to the cruise line you own along with the first three letters of your last name, Mr. Penlin. And I would bet my bakery that this here key would fit one of the kitchen doors on the North Queen."

Heath stared at the silver key. His mind began to race. "You're insane," he snapped at Momma Peach. "My name isn't Penlin. My name is—"

"Heath Penlin," Michelle interrupted. "Don't lie to us, okay? The best thing you can do is help yourself out by telling the truth."

"And," Momma Peach said, laying the trap, "you'd better make sure your words match what your hired snake confessed to Detective Chan."

Heath stared at Momma Peach. Had Marc loosened his tongue to a cop? Surely not. But he could not be sure. How well did he really know Marc? Not well enough. After all, he did travel all the way to Alaska to kill the man. "Okay, fine, my name is Heath Penlin," Heath caved in. "I own the Blue Wave cruise line, too. I came here to find a man who was hired to sabotage my ship and...speak with him," Heath quickly lied.

"That's not what I heard you tell him over the phone," Mitchel informed Heath and carefully explained how he had listened in on the conversation between him and

Marc. Heath felt the bottom drop out of his stomach. "Speak the truth," Mitchel warned Heath.

Heath wanted to bolt but knew his chance of escape was minimal. Even if he did manage to escape from the dining room and make it outside, he would have a deadly killer to contend with in the rain. His best chance was to play ball with these amateurs for a while until he could devise a clever survival plan. "The North Queen is a cursed ship, it's true," he spoke in a slow voice. "It's costing me a fortune to keep the ship insured and even more money to maintain the ship's upkeep. My sister," Heath decided to let out some rope, "bought the ship from a shady European dealer. This was...before I joined the company."

"Before you got out of prison, you mean," Momma Peach fired at Heath. "Listen, boy, we know all about your prison record. So don't talk smoothly to me. You are nothing but a sewer rat. Oh, give me strength not to slap this man into the next decade."

Heath grew silent. He worked his thoughts into a tight fist and then spoke. "I took a wrong turn in my life and served my time," he said through gritted teeth. "When I was released from prison, my sister decided to bring me into the family business. I was more than happy to have a job, but what I didn't know was that my sister had other plans for me and the North Queen." Heath steadied his mind. "The company was suffering financially when I came on board. I convinced my sister to let me invest our limited funds into the ship, not realizing she was just a cursed vessel through and through...horrible mistake on my part, I admit. No matter how much money and energy I invested into the North Queen...she just seemed to get worse. We're talking about a great sum of money here, people. I spruced up the North Queen and made her the equal of any cruise ship running across the waves. But...things kept going wrong."

"Like murder," Momma Peach pointed out. "We know about Mr. Minson, rest his soul."

Heath calmly took a bite of eggs. "Minson was murdered by the same man you found dead this morning," he said, forcing his voice to remain level. "Minson was an undercover FBI agent." Heath swallowed his food. "Minson also dated my sister and introduced her to Marc. The two of them devised a plan to sink the ship at sea, collect the insurance money, sell off the cruise line, and retire in Italy, rich and fat. Later, I found out that my sister was planning to pin the crime directly on me."

"Keep talking, boy," Momma Peach ordered Heath.

"My sister was letting me invest money into the North Queen in order to increase the value of the ship while her crooked FBI boyfriend began running weapons using its cargo hold. At the same time, Marc, the man you found dead, was sabotaging the ship's electrical system, plumbing system, navigational system, you name it. This was being done to make it appear that I was somehow failing in my mission to improve the company's finances, even though my efforts had turned an aging boat into a grand ship." Heath continued, believing his lies were being accepted. "Minson planned on making me more than just the scapegoat for the crime. He was going to kill me, make it appear as a suicide, and leave a note explaining that my financial woes over the North Queen led me to end my life. This is, of course, after he ran enough guns to Europe to please his bosses."

Momma Peach reached down, picked up her pocketbook, stood up, walked around the table to Heath, and began beating him over the head. "Stop your lying," she yelled and walloped Heath over the head. "Your sister was found dead and her death was ruled a suicide, you dog-faced liar! Now you better start telling the truth before I put you on the front porch hogtied so we can feed you to the killer!"

Heath covered his head with his arms and hunkered down under the blows. "Get this woman off of me...lady! Stop hitting me...you're insane!"

"Insane this," Momma Peach cried out and smacked Heath mightily upside the head with her pocketbook. "I can't stand liars! No, sir and no ma'am! Especially not a low-down, yellow-belly, no-good-for-nothing flea-bag like you!" Momma Peach walloped Heath with her pocketbook again. "You better start speaking the truth, or I am going to beat you into yesteryear!"

"Okay, okay," Heath yelled, "I lied...okay? Nothing I said was the truth."

Momma Peach stopped hitting Heath with her purse and backed away. She walked back to her chair and sat down, breathing hard. Her eyes bored into his. "Talk, boy."

"The North Queen is a lemon, that much is true. My sister was foolish for buying that ship. The electrical system was shot, the navigational system outdated, the plumbing in chaos. My sister was on the losing end and sinking fast but she refused to stop investing money into the North Queen. She was determined to turn its fortunes. And sure, on the outside, the ship looked fancy enough, but the guts of the ship were rusted and no good. She was sending us into bankruptcy for a ship that was never going to make it out of the harbor."

"So you killed your own sister, is that it?" Momma Peach asked. She narrowed her eyes and looked at Heath. "Speak the truth, boy. We know your renovations didn't begin on the North Queen until after you arrived. Don't make me go crazy on you again!"

Heath swallowed. His lies were getting him nowhere. He looked desperately at them, trying to formulate a position.

"Your prison buddies needed a ship to haul drugs and

guns on, right?" Michelle asked Heath. "There was no crooked gun-running boyfriend. You invested money into the ship, you created private dining rooms, hallways, smoking rooms. You designed a ship perfect for stowing hidden cargo and hiding criminals."

Momma Peach nodded her head. "And your sister found out what your plans were and you killed her."

"I bet Mr. Minson was an undercover law enforcement agent after all. And you killed him," Michelle added.

"Alright, enough," Heath hit the dining table with his fists. "It's true, okay? I was using the North Queen to run drugs and guns for some very powerful men I met in prison. But," Heath gritted his teeth, "the ship was a lemon, as I stated. I kept being dogged with one problem after the next...electrical...plumbing...engine room problems...I sank money into sprucing up the ship and tried to cut corners on the other stuff, and all those mechanical issues turned into a huge problem. Which didn't go over well with the men I was working for...men who had given me a large sum of money to turn the North Queen into a luxury ship for their use." Heath ran his hands through his hair. "After I discovered Minson was a mole, the men I work for ordered me to kill him, sink the North Queen, collect the insurance money, and pay them back the money I owed them...or die." Heath looked at Momma Peach. "I had other plans."

Momma Peach stared across the table at Heath. The

cobra was rearing its ugly head. Outside, the rain continued to fall.

Far away, hidden in the dense underbrush in a small cave, a dark figure slept in silence, anxious for the day to fade and the night to awaken.

CHAPTER SEVEN

*H*eath put down his fork and folded his arms. What did he have to lose in telling the truth? If he died then maybe one of the people sitting at the dining room table might be able to reveal his plan, which would really be a slap in the face of his enemies—people who betrayed him when push came to shove. Heath didn't like being betrayed. "I'll tell you what my plan was. I hired Marc myself to sabotage the North Queen and—"

"Wait a minute," Momma Peach snapped. "Go back to your sister, boy."

Heath narrowed his eyes. "My sister agreed to let Minson work undercover on the North Queen in order to save her own butt. In truth, she was innocent, but she betrayed me. I...didn't kill her personally." His face twisted in a pitiless way. "My sister was a

143

very...depressed woman who met a very...unfortunate end."

"Hold me down!" Momma Peach hollered. She shot to her feet and tried to run at Heath, but Sam managed to grab her in time. "Hold me down, hold me down, hold me down!"

Heath watched Sam help Momma Peach back to her chair. "Lady, my life was on the line. The people I was working for are extremely powerful and deadly." Heath waited until Momma Peach sat down before he continued. He sure didn't feel like being beaten with a pocketbook again. "I hired Marc to begin sabotaging the North Queen," he said again.

"Why?" Michelle demanded.

Heath showed a hideous grin. "I don't like being betrayed or bullied. I don't like having my life threatened. The men who were strong-arming me thought they could make me the fall guy for their schemes, so they needed to be taught a lesson. And they will be a taught a lesson...if I survive this nightmare."

"What do you mean?" Michelle asked in a tough tone that was evidence of her long experience with interrogations.

"You see, I made sure Marc Stravinsky would be the one linked to the criminals behind all this. My name will be clean."

"I see," Momma Peach said. "You want the authorities to believe it was your thug's buddies behind the acts of sabotage."

Heath nodded his head. "Exactly. I'll claim I was being forced against my will to turn the North Queen into a drug- and gun-running ship. I'll prove that the men I work for threatened my life and the ship, which is certainly true. I'll prove that every time I attempted to break free, the men I worked for attacked me and my ship, keeping me imprisoned in a web of criminal activities, which is... not exactly true. And in the end," Marc grinned again, "Boom."

"Boom?" Able asked.

"Boom," Heath promised. "One last voyage out to sea and boom, the North Queen sinks. But I'm not a monster, you see. I orchestrated that kitchen fire in order to prevent the passengers from boarding the ship, which went exactly according to plan. I needed the authorities to see that the suspicious kitchen fire was started on the same day the North Queen was scheduled to set sail. And then," Heath said in a pleased voice, "I wanted the authorities to see exactly what you'll see if you ever get out of this miserable lodge and check a newspaper...the North Queen later sailed away from the port for a routine maintenance voyage and tragically sank at sea...with drugs and guns aboard, of course."

"You're a rat," Momma Peach said, resisting the urge to smack Heath.

"Am I?" Heath asked. "I deliberately scheduled the North Queen to set sail while fully loaded down with guns. That's only a couple days from now. A major gun shipment arrived a week ago. I took some heat and was ordered to reroute the cruise to deliver the guns...or die. I expected this, of course, and worked Marc into the formula, hiring him to ensure that the kitchen fire would keep the ship docked. The cruise was canceled and the North Queen was ordered to remain docked until inspected and cleared." Heath looked down at his plate, idly pushing around a last bite. Despite his choices in life, he was surely the victor in this situation and victory was sweet. "But then Marc panicked the day he started the kitchen fire because Dave Charleston spotted him."

"Dave Charleston?" Michelle asked.

"Dave Charleston is a very deadly man. He's an expert weapons man and would kill you just for sport. The men I was working for always sent Dave to pass information to me and Marc. Marc was a tough guy, but he was scared of the men I was working for, and no match for Dave Charleston." Heath paused, collected his thoughts, and continued. "Dave Charleston had slipped us that key in the matchbox because my bosses wanted the kitchen sabotaged after they made the next weapons delivery. Kitchen equipment on a cruise ship is expensive, you see.

A fantastic way to delay in port while various...special cargo are loaded. But Dave didn't just pass the key to Marc and leave town, as usual. He stuck around, apparently to make sure the departure went off without a hitch, and that's when he spotted Marc. So Marc slipped the box of matches he used to start the fire, along with the kitchen key, into your pocket." Heath pointed at Momma Peach, "Because he was worried Dave might catch up to him and if he was caught with the matches...lights out. Lady," Heath pointed at Momma Peach again, "you were in the wrong place at the wrong time." He chuckled.

"Do you think you're some kind of genius?" Momma Peach hollered, incensed. "Give this boy a gold star and send him to brain surgery school. Oh, give me the strength."

Heath was growing tired of Momma Peach. "Lady, I came here to kill Marc, which would spare your life. I knew Marc was getting messy, meaning he could have caused a lot more problems for me. I also knew he was intent on killing me because I could tie him to the North Queen, which meant my bosses would have no reason to protect him."

"How nice of you," Momma Peach told Heath and shook her head. "You came all the way up here to Alaska to murder a man and spare little ol' Momma Peach. Oh, you're a real saint, boy. I guess you didn't expect to become the hunted, huh?"

"No," Heath admitted, "I didn't. And I'm on a strict timeline. Being delayed was not part of the plan. The North Queen is going to set sail in two days whether I'm there or not. If I'm not at the dock the day she sets sail, then my plan will backfire."

"Remote detonation?" Michelle queried, looking at Heath. "Is that how you plan to detonate the explosives you planted on the ship?"

Heath grew silent and finally nodded his head. "Yes," he said. "In two days, ten wealthy and deadly men from Europe, America, Africa, Canada, Mexico and Asia are going to board the North Queen and sail out to international waters while they discuss the creation of a global criminal network using cruise ships as a means of operation. The North Queen, you must understand, was just a way to test the waters, so to speak." Heath looked at Michelle. "I'm doing the world a favor by getting rid of some very ugly people."

"But wouldn't you be placing your life in danger?" Able asked Heath. "If you go public with your plan...I mean, I'm sure those ten men will leave cronies behind. So there will be other people who will not be pleased with you."

"Ah," Heath said and nodded his head, "maybe not. Maybe," he said in a pleased voice, "there are some men who want the North Queen sunk who have offered me protection."

"Oh, you're playing sides," Momma Peach said and leaned back in her chair. "You're a sneaky one."

"I'm smart," Heath snapped. "I was betrayed once when a person I called my friend left me holding the bag for a bank robbery I didn't want any part of. I swore that I would never be betrayed again. When the North Queen sets sail and I sink her, the authorities are going to find tons of illegal guns at the bottom of the sea, guns destined to arm terrorist groups around the globe. They're going to uncover how a rogue hired gun, the thug Marc Stravinsky, planted a bomb on the North Queen, leaving me in the clear. When I tell the FBI everything I know about the bad men who forced me to do their dirty work," here he snickered under his breath, "I'm going to get no more than a slap on the wrist. No prison time. And then I'll be free to collect my insurance money. Then I'm going to sail the cruise line and vanish into thin air."

"Nice and tidy, huh?" Momma Peach asked.

"Until now," Heath confessed. "I should have killed Marc instead of letting him trail you to Alaska. So what if you had the matchbox? But Marc insisted and I caved in. And now I'm trapped."

"Why are you telling us your plans?" Sam wondered.

"If I die," Heath told Sam, "and one of you lives, at least I'll still be able to get some form of revenge. Can you understand that?"

"And if you live, you're going to prison," Michelle promised Heath.

"No," Heath corrected Michelle, "I will never let prison bars close in front of my face again." And with those words, Heath stood up. "I'll be in my room. Don't worry, I'm not going to run. Where would I run to? If Marc Stravinsky was strangled to death, that tells me this killer is very dangerous. Besides, I'm not exactly an outdoors person. I wouldn't stand a chance."

"Go back to your room, then," Michelle said and nodded her head at the dining room doorway. "If you do run, I'm not responsible for your safety."

Heath walked out of the dining room. As he made his way upstairs, he whispered, "It looks like I'm on my own." He had no intention of telling the others his true plan, which was to wire together a crude radio; he had learned many useful skills in prison. The radio would be capable of signaling an outpost in the town two hours away, where an associate waited for his signal and would come fetch him. Heath knew he could not risk stealing supplies to make the radio until after the others had gone to bed. Pleased, he stole back to his room and locked the door, not knowing that he would be dead before nightfall.

"What do you think?" Sam asked everyone. He took a sip of his coffee. "I sat here and listened to every word Penlin said, same as you. You managed to back him out of his lies, but I wonder if he confessed the whole truth?"

"You sure gave him a beating," Able told Momma Peach. "Remind me to never back talk you."

"I would never hit you with my pocketbook, baby, because you're a real decent kind of fella that I respect," Momma Peach promised Able. She smoothed down her hair under her headwrap and shook her head. "My, my, what a tangled web we're in. The criminal mind never ceases to amaze me. Here we have a man who thinks he's being mighty clever when in truth he's dug his own pit to fall in." Momma Peach picked up her coffee mug and took a sip of coffee, but it had gone cold. She shuddered. "Meanwhile, we have a killer running loose who may or may not be the son of a man named Dr. Dennerton. My, oh my, what a tangled web these Alaskan woods are wrapped in."

Mitchel stood up and walked to the dining room window. He pulled back the curtain a little further and looked outside. He could barely see the lake. "Rain will be falling like this all day, heavy and steady. The land gets soaking wet when we get cloud cover like this. I used to enjoy mornings like this one...still do, I guess. I always liked how the rainclouds seemed to sit up in the trees and change the ground into a peaceful...well, dream world, really. When the world is wet, it seems to me, the mind can rest and dream easier."

"Are you okay, Mr. Mitchel?" Momma Peach asked worriedly.

"Oh, depressed, I guess. I had forgotten how I treated Dr. Dennerton's son. I can handle men like Mr. Penlin. I expect bad behavior from men like that. But I won't tolerate my own behavior, on the other side of the coin. I...had a fury in my heart the day I ran Dr. Dennerton's wife and son out into the snow. I nearly...killed that boy."

Sam stood up and walked over to Mitchel. He put his arm around Mitchel's shoulder. "Sometimes, my friend," he said in a caring voice, "when someone we love is threatened, well, something deep inside of us...an instinct...breaks loose and reacts. You can't blame yourself for protecting your wife who was suffering from cancer. I would have acted in the same way you did...only, maybe, I might have killed Dr. Dennerton's son instead of letting him run free, after a threat like that."

Mitchel looked over into Sam's eyes. He saw a caring friend. "Thank you, Sam."

"Anytime," Sam smiled. "Now, the important thing is to focus on the killer and worry about Penlin later. I'm sure that man's mind is running around a wheel trying to get somewhere, but right now he doesn't seem to be a threat."

"What can we do?" Mitchel asked Sam.

"Secure the lodge," Sam stated. "I have a bad feeling when night falls the electricity is going to go out."

"I have a generator in the basement," Mitchel pointed out. "We'll have lights regardless."

"Good," Sam said. He saw relief wash through Momma Peach's eyes. "We need to secure the doors, post guards, set traps, anything we can think of."

Able squeezed Michelle's hand. "Don't be afraid," he told her and then realized he was talking to a woman who could kick the teeth out of a grizzly bear's mouth. "Never mind, that was a stupid thing to say," he mumbled.

"No," Michelle begged Able, "don't hold back your concern for me. I want you to be worried about me and comfort me because the truth is, I am scared. I'm always scared. I might not show it the way other women do, but deep down inside of my...heart...I get scared. I want to be held and told everything is going to be okay." Michelle looked at Able with pleading eyes. "Tell me everything is going to be okay, please?"

Able wrapped his arm around Michelle and pulled her close. "Everything is going to be okay," he promised, even though he wasn't sure if he believed his promise. He looked at Momma Peach. Momma Peach simply nodded her head and straightened the cloth covering her hair.

***

Mitchel walked into the kitchen and found Momma Peach standing alone. "Are you okay, Momma Peach?"

Momma Peach kept her eyes on the oval window. She stood silent and listened to the rain. "The rain is so peaceful," she told Mitchel. "I love the rain. Oh, maybe not all the time, but sometimes I love to go outside, sit on my front porch in my favorite rocking chair, and watch a rain shower pass by. I love the smell of the earth after the rain stops. God's precious earth smells rinsed clean. All the bad is washed away and beauty shines."

Mitchel walked over to the refrigerator in the kitchen and pulled out a root beer. "Most folks don't see rain that way. But we old timers, do, huh, Momma Peach?"

"We sure do, baby," Momma Peach told Mitchel and allowed a gentle smile to touch her lips. "Well now, I better get back to baking my peach pie. I've been doing a whole lot of thinking and decided baking will help rest my brain a minute."

Mitchel studied the circular kitchen table in the corner of the kitchen. The table was covered with flour, spices, and lots of love. Momma Peach walked over to the table and began forming a pie crust with her soft hands. "Root beer?" he asked.

"No thank you, baby," Momma Peach told Mitchel. She drew in a deep breath of spices and the cedarwood smell of the kitchen cabinets. The kitchen air reminded her of her bakery back home in Georgia. Yet this log cabin kitchen in Alaska was somehow becoming a part of her as well. Even though the lodge still felt somewhat unfamiliar, with its rough-hewn walls and Mrs. Mitchel's old quilts and those dramatic mountain views, it was beginning to take root in her heart. "Let me tell you a secret...I sneaked me a root beer earlier," she said and tossed Mitchel a wink.

Mitchel smiled. "Nothing like a good, cold root beer."

"Yes sir, indeed," Momma Peach agreed. "Now, tell me, how are the fortifications coming along while I've been baking?"

Mitchel leaned against the kitchen counter and sipped his root beer. "All the downstairs windows are nailed shut. All the doors are reinforced. The basement is secure. Only a tank could get into this lodge." Mitchel shook his head. "I sure don't like being forced to barricade myself in my own home like this. I'm starting to feel suffocated."

"We're bait, baby. We have to draw the snake to us," Momma Peach reminded Mitchel. "When the daylight vanishes and that dark arrives, I ain't sure what's going to happen. But I have been doing some thinking and I believe the killer murdered that fella named Marc as a way to show off his skills. The killer wants us to know just how deadly he is."

"I never considered that."

"The killer could have attacked anyone of us at any time," Momma Peach continued, using a well-worn rolling pin to roll out the pie crust with practiced hands. "Instead, the killer wants to play games. That's why he slashes the tires on them vehicles outside and cuts the phone line. The killer wants us trapped inside of a sick little game." Momma Peach continued to roll the pie crust thinner, her brow wrinkled in thought. "The killer also killed that fella Marc as a warning."

"A warning?"

"For us not to run," Momma Peach stated in a serious voice. "If we run, we're dead, that's the message, baby. I'm sure I'm right, yes, sir and yes ma'am. So don't feel crammed up in this here lovely lodge. We're safe inside here. We're safe as long as we stay together."

Mitchel looked down at the cold bottle of root beer in his hand. "The older I get, the more helpless I feel at times. It has nothing to do with locked doors or guns, either. I was in the Army during the Korean War. I was young, strong...and a bit reckless. I never backed down from a fight and met the enemy head-on. My attitude was the reason I took a bullet to my chest...nearly died, too. After I was discharged, I settled down inside and found Jesus. Soon after, I met my wife and she helped me focus on our future. Now...the future seems...lonely."

Momma Peach had finished rolling out the pie crust. She looked at Mitchel. The sadness consuming the man's eyes broke her heart into a million little pieces. "I understand, baby. When my husband left me to go to heaven, I felt awfully lonely...angry...even betrayed. I sure couldn't understand why the good Lord would take away my husband so young. And I sure didn't know how I was going to face a whole lot of lonely nights. But in time, I surrendered to the good Lord's will and accepted His strength. Oh, there are still nights that are tough to get through, but morning comes and so do smiles and laughter."

Mitchel sipped his root beer, his eyes focused on the distant trees through the rain outside the window. "Momma Peach, I'm nearing the end of my path. You still have many good years left. I've lived a long, full life. I'm ready to go home to Jesus and be with my wife. And when it's my time, the Lord will call me home. Between now and then I don't want to live my life as a coward. It's not right for a man to hide himself away instead of facing a threat head-on."

Momma Peach didn't know what to say. She understood Mitchel's loneliness and respected the man deeply for his convictions. But how did he intend to confront this faceless threat? "Mr. Mitchel—" she began to speak but stopped when Heath appeared at the doorway to the kitchen. "What is it, boy?" she asked and glanced meaningfully at her pocketbook sitting on the kitchen counter.

"It'll be dark soon," Heath told Momma Peach in a cool

157

voice. "I've been watching you guys barricade us in this rat hole all day."

"Watch your mouth, boy!" Momma Peach snarled at Heath. "Have some respect for Mr. Mitchel and his lodge. Don't make me beat some manners into that ugly head of yours. I'm ready for a fight! Oh, give me strength, Mr. Mitchel."

Heath glanced at Mitchel. Mitchel motioned at the gun resting in a leather holster attached to his belt and Heath took the hint, stepping back. "I'm not here to fight, lady. I just want to know what the plan is. We can't stay barricaded in here forever. One of you should try and reach the sheriff." Heath needed to distract the others so he could search out components for his radio, and had decided this was the best option: send a hapless victim out on the long trek into town, and hopefully distract the killer into the bargain.

"Be my guest," Momma Peach told Heath. "Take a hike."

"Not me," Heath said. He pointed at Mitchel. "You should be the one to go, old man. You know the roads around here the best, and you're responsible for our safety. I doubt the killer will waste his time on an old bag like you, since—"

Momma Peach struck the table with her fist and then charged at Heath. Heath tried to back away but bumped into the doorframe. Momma Peach dived toward him, tackled him down to the floor, and began beating his head into the wood floorboards. "I'll beat some respect into your head yet!" she yelled.

Heath struggled to break free from Momma Peach, clawing at her hands around his neck. "Get this crazy woman off of me!"

Sam, Michelle, and Able came running. They saw Momma Peach beating Heath's head into the floor. "Get him, Momma Peach!" Michelle murmured, sure that Mr. Penlin deserved it.

Sam sighed. He walked over to Momma Peach and dragged her off the man. "Easy now, Momma Peach. Save your strength."

Momma Peach snorted. "That rat needs to be taught some manners, yes, sir and yes ma'am," she growled and let Sam help her stand up. "Mr. Mitchel deserves respect, oh yes he does."

Heath crawled to his feet and began rubbing the back of his head. "Lady, you're insane!" he yelled.

"I'll show you insane, punk!" Momma Peach screamed and tried to charge at Heath again. Sam grabbed her. "Let me go baby, because I have some business to attend to and I ain't looking to get any change back! I'm going to make a full deposit on that punk's head!"

"Easy now," Sam begged Momma Peach. "Don't waste your energy."

Heath glowered at Momma Peach, retreating to the hallway and staying well away from Michelle and the others. It was clear to him that he would have to wait a little longer before he could put his escape plan into action. "I'll be in my room," he snarled and stormed away.

"I've gotta get out of here," he told himself as he headed for the stairs. He regretted telling those idiots everything but was certain the FBI would suppress any statement they made concerning what he told them. His information would be too important, the FBI had bigger fish to fry and his testimony would seal the deal. But he was still worried. "If I don't reach the dock in two days, it won't matter. I'll be a dead man no matter what," he snapped to the empty air.

Heath hurried upstairs to his room. As he walked into his room he was suddenly pulled back, and a burning pain seared and squeezed his neck. A thin wire was wrapped tightly around his throat and he heard a foot kick the room door shut. He began fighting to break free from the thin wire, but the more he fought and kicked his heels against the floor, the more his attacker tightened his grip. The last thought Heath Penlin had before dying was how the sounds of the struggle and even his death throes would have no chance of being heard over the hard rain that continued to pour down outside.

"That jerk," Momma Peach said and after a deep breath, returned to her pie crust, lifting and placing it carefully in the pie dish on the table. "Baby," she told Sam, "you should have let me beat some sense into that boy."

"He's not worth it," Sam told Momma Peach. He shook his head. "We're secure. Just in time, too. The last of the daylight is fading away."

Mitchel finished off his root beer. "So, now we...wait," he said. The kitchen grew silent. The sound of the heavy falling rain filled the air. Finally, Mitchel spoke again. "Root beer anyone?"

"I'll have a root beer," Michelle raised her hand.

"Me, too," Able added.

"Make it three," Sam said. "Momma Peach?"

"No thanks, baby," Momma Peach told Sam. She looked up at the ceiling. "I can't stand bad manners, no, sir and no ma'am."

Mitchel opened the refrigerator and brought out three bottles of root beer. He handed them out and then walked over to Momma Peach and rubbed her shoulders. "If my wife was alive today she would adopt you as her own, Momma Peach. You're some kind of woman."

Momma Peach blushed. "Aw, I ain't much."

161

"Yes, you are," Mitchel objected and kissed Momma Peach on her cheek. "You're amazing."

Momma Peach looked at Mitchel. She looked into a pair of loving eyes that warmed her heart. Sure, the world was full of sleazebags, but the world was also full of Mr. Mitchels and Mr. Sams. "Thank—" Momma Peach hushed her mouth. She heard a suspicious sound float into the kitchen from the front lobby. No one else seemed to hear the sound.

"What is it?" Sam asked, alarmed.

Michelle whipped out her gun. "Momma Peach?"

"Someone is in the front lobby," Momma Peach whispered. "And it ain't Penlin. I know the sounds everyone in this lodge makes."

"No one can get into the lodge. We secured—" Able began to speak. Momma Peach raised her finger to her lip. "Oh, okay," he finished in a whisper.

Sam fetched out his gun and looked at Michelle. "Ready?"

"Let's move," Michelle told Sam. "I'll lead. You cover me. Mitchel, you take the rear. Able, you follow behind and protect Momma Peach."

"With my life," Able promised and took Momma Peach's hand.

Momma Peach picked up a sharp kitchen knife with her left hand. "Let's go, baby," she whispered to Able and followed Michelle, Sam, and Mitchel out of the kitchen. Her blood grew cold. Something was amiss.

Michelle eased into the front lobby with her gun at the ready. Her eyes immediately spotted Heath Penlin's body lying in a heap at the foot of the stairs. "Man down," she called over her shoulder to Sam. "Cover me." Michelle ran over to Heath and bent down to check the man for any signs of life. The thin red mark at his neck looked sickeningly fresh. "He's been strangled," she said and shot to her feet. "Just like Marc Stravinsky."

Sam rushed over to Michelle and pointed his gun up the staircase. "How?" he demanded in frustration. "We're boarded up in here tighter than ticks on a dog."

Momma Peach let go of Able's hand and walked over to Heath's dead body. She looked down into the man's face and shook her head. "All of your planning came to nothing, didn't it? You came to a miserable end, too." Momma Peach closed her eyes and whispered a prayer and then walked to the front counter and placed the kitchen knife down with a shaky hand. "One down, five to go," she said in a miserable, scared voice and pointed at Mitchel. "Mitchel will be the last one to die."

Sam lowered his gun. "Mitchel, are you sure we secured every door and window?" he asked desperately.

"I'm sure," Mitchel reassured Sam. "I don't know how anyone could have gotten into the lodge from outside without us knowing."

Able walked over to Michelle and took her hand. "We can walk out of here."

"No," Michelle said, "not in the dark. Not in the rain."

"If we stay here, we might die," Able pleaded. "If we leave as a group we can make it."

"No, son," Mitchel informed Able, "we won't make it. If the killer made it into the lodge, they'll surely follow us onto the road or into the woods, where they'll pick us off one by one." Mitchel walked over to the front door and checked the lock and then focused his attention on the fire burning in the fireplace. "We're at the mercy of a killer," he told everyone, "and there isn't a thing in the world that we can do about it. But I do know panic isn't an option. We have to remain calm and level-headed."

"I like the way you think," Momma Peach spoke up. She studied the lobby with careful eyes and began wondering how the killer managed to enter the lodge without being heard. Surely, she thought, there had to be some kind of hidden entrance that Mr. Mitchel was unaware of. "Mr. Mitchel, baby, ask your mind to search your lodge and see if you might have missed a room or a door or a window, anything. Your lodge isn't the size of a mansion, but it also isn't a little matchbox. There's enough room to hide a few elephants up in here."

Mitchel shook his head. "Momma Peach, I've lived in this lodge for many, many years. I know every inch of this lodge by heart."

Sam rubbed his left hand through his hair. "How?" he asked himself. "How did the killer get inside?"

Michelle let go of Able's hand, bent down, and ran her fingers over the bottom stair of the staircase. "Wet," she said. Michelle felt the lobby floor. "Dry. The killer didn't come through the lobby."

"Which means the killer went back upstairs," Mitchel said in relief. "The only way downstairs is the staircase. If we all stand guard in the lobby, we might stand a chance."

"No," Momma Peach said and shook her head. "The killer will find another way inside." Momma Peach walked over the fireplace and warmed her shaking hands. Her mind raced as she murmured to herself. "Momma Peach, you better start putting that mind of yours to work and calm yourself down, girl. There's a killer loose and you ain't gonna become grave bait for some insane psycho. Now get that mind of yours working."

Upstairs, a man dressed in a black tactical raincoat and pants grinned as he listened to the conversation taking place down in the lobby. "That's right," he hissed, "talk it over and see what you want to do. I'll be waiting for you." The man eased back down the hallway and vanished.

Able took Michelle's hand and pulled her over to the front desk. He looked into her worried face and saw the fear lingering in her eyes. "I know I'm not a cop," he told Michelle, "but I think it might be smart if I carried a gun."

Michelle hesitated. She was falling deeply in love with Able, but the thought of Able carrying a gun terrified her. The poor man still tripped over his own feet. But was this truly the right time to offend a sweet man by discussing his clumsiness? Surely survival was more important. "Okay," she reluctantly agreed. "You can carry my back-up gun that I put in Momma Peach's pocketbook."

Sam kept his eyes on the staircase. "How?" he kept asking himself over and over.

Mitchel walked over to Momma Peach and looked into the fire burning in the fireplace. "It's going to be a long night, Momma Peach."

"Yes, baby, the night is sure gonna try to wear me down," Momma Peach agreed and said no more. Outside, the last of daylight evaporated above the steep hills and the lake down below. Above, the sky pulled the dangerous night out from behind a heavy curtain.

CHAPTER EIGHT

*S*am wasn't satisfied. "We boarded up this lodge tighter than Fort Knox," he told Momma Peach in a frustrated voice. "How did the killer get inside without being heard?"

Momma Peach watched Sam pace back and forth in front of the fireplace. "I don't know baby, but there's only one place we haven't explored. Michelle says the killer came from upstairs, which means somewhere upstairs there's an entrance or a hidden door that no one is aware of." Momma Peach raised her eyes to the ceiling. "You know what we have to do, Mr. Sam?"

Sam looked at Michelle. Michelle nodded her head. "We have to go upstairs. Able and Mitchel can stay in the lobby."

Able nervously fiddled with the gun he was holding. The

gun felt dangerous and menacing. "Sure, we'll stay here. If we see the killer, we'll fire off a warning shot."

"I'll do more than fire a warning shot," Mitchel assured everyone. He walked behind the front counter and positioned himself. "We'll secure the lobby. You guys go check upstairs. If you run into any trouble, fire a few shots and we'll come running."

Sam hesitated. The killer could be hiding anywhere upstairs, waiting. "Okay," he finally agreed. "But Momma Peach, you stay down here in the lobby with—"

"No, baby," Momma Peach interrupted Sam, "I'm going upstairs with you. If Michelle goes, I go. No arguments."

Sam wanted to argue with Momma Peach, but the look in the woman's determined eyes told him that attempting to argue would only waste time and energy. He stood silent for a few seconds and listened to the rain fall and the winds howl. "Let's move."

"I'll take the lead. Sam, you follow second and Momma Peach, you cover the rear," Michelle said. She felt scared. The unknown awaited upstairs. The killer could be concealed in any room, any corner, any shadow, ready to attack. She wasn't even sure what to look for upstairs. More windows and doors? All Michelle knew was that they had to locate the hidden entrance and secure it. "Let's move."

Michelle carefully began to ease up the staircase with her

finger poised on the trigger of her gun. Sam followed behind her and last came Momma Peach, gripping her pocketbook and watching Michelle with worried eyes. When Michelle reached the top of the stairs and stepped into the hallway, Momma Peach hustled Sam up the stairs so as not to lose sight of her.

"Clear," Michelle whispered, staring down the eerily quiet hallway. Sam and Momma Peach joined her. Momma Peach saw every room door closed tight. "The reading room and the game room are the last two rooms at the end of the hallway," she said. "I personally locked the windows in those rooms. Sam locked all the windows in the guest rooms. I'm not sure where we're supposed to look." Michelle stared down the long, deserted hallway and felt cold chills race down her spine. The hallway no longer appeared cozy or inviting. Instead, it had transformed into an ugly mouth that had been scraped raw by an agonized, dying scream.

"We'll check the reading room and the game room first and then work our way through the guest rooms," Sam said. He locked his eyes on the two doors stationed at the end of the hallway. Light was coming from under each door. "Michelle, did we leave the lights on in each room?" he asked.

Momma Peach focused on the stream of light flooding out from under the doors to the reading room and the game room. Suddenly a memory flashed into her mind. "I was helping Mr. Michel downstairs earlier, baby," Momma Peach told Michelle in a low, urgent whisper. "I ain't familiar with the game room or the reading room, but I stuck my head into each room last night just to take a quick glance, that was all. I do remember seeing a wood-burning stove in the reading room."

Sam looked at Momma Peach and struggled to understand her statement. Then, his frustrated mind understood. "Of course, the stove pipe," he said in a hoarse whisper. "The stove pipe leads straight up to the roof."

Michelle closed her eyes and walked down the hallway in her mind's eye; she opened the door leading into the reading room and spotted the old wood-burning stove. She focused on the stove pipe attached to the stove. The pipe wasn't large enough for a man to fit through. But maybe the hole in the roof was. "The killer would have to remove the stove pipe and come down through the hole in the roof, assuming the hole is large enough. Even if it wasn't, the killer could easily enlarge the hole with a saw without being heard because of the rain and wind."

"Only one way to find out," Sam said and pointed down the hallway. "Detective Chan, lead the way. Momma Peach and I have your back."

Michelle drew in a deep breath, steadied her nerves, and maneuvered down the hallway, passing each closed door with extreme caution, expecting the killer to burst out from one of the closed doors at her at any second. When she reached the door leading into the game room, she paused. "Sam," she whispered and motioned to the right side of the door, "station yourself right here. When I kick open the door, run in right behind me. Momma Peach, you stay out in the hallway until we yell all clear."

"Okay, baby," Momma Peach promised. She watched Michelle position her body in front of the door and Sam slide over into position. She tightened her grip on her purse and prayed.

Michelle drew back her right leg, brought her gun up into a firing position, and then kicked the door open with one swift, powerful kick. The door exploded open, flying off its hinges. Michelle raced into the room. As she did, she spotted a black-clad figure disappearing through a wide hole that had been cut into the ceiling. She dropped down onto her knee, aimed her gun at the legs and knees that were still visible, and fired off three rounds. The figure scrambled for a moment at the edge of the hole, stunned or unbalanced by the gunfire, but then vanished into the ceiling.

Sam ran into the reading room. "There!" Michelle yelled and pointed up at the hole. Sam raised his gun and fired off five rounds.

"Oh, give me strength," Momma Peach begged, cringing from the sound of the gunfire. She heard footsteps, spun

171

around, and saw Mitchel and Able racing down the hallway.

"What's happening?" Able yelled and nearly tripped over his own feet. Mitchel caught him just in the nick of time.

Sam stuck his head out of the reading room. "We're okay," he hollered out into the hallway. "The killer removed the pipe connected to the wood stove and cut a hole in the ceiling. That's how he got in. My guess is there's another hole, equal to the one in the reading room ceiling, cut into the roof. No rain is falling in this room, so the hole must not be right above us."

"Well, I'll be," Mitchel said and shook his head. "Isn't that clever."

"The rain and the wind must have covered the sounds the killer made breaking in," Sam told Mitchel. He looked at Momma Peach. "Are you okay, Momma Peach?"

Momma Peach nodded her head and walked into the reading room. She looked up and spotted an ugly, dark hole in the ceiling and the pockmarks from a few bullets that had gone astray. "My, my," she said and lowered her face and looked around the cozy, warm reading room. Two hand-carved bookshelves stood against the north and south walls, lined with delicious-looking books to devour on a rainy night. A wide red and brown carpet covered most of the hardwood floor, and the room had four green and white reading chairs positioned around the wood stove. A metal wood bin was shoved up into one corner, full of logs. The room had only one window, covered with a thick brown drape. Momma Peach walked over to the window, pulled back the drape and looked out into the dark night. "My, my," she said again.

Mitchel walked into the reading room with Able. Able ran over to Michelle and took her into his arms. "Are you okay?" he asked.

Michelle nodded. "I saw the killer escaping up through the hole. I fired off three rounds. I'm not sure if I hit my target or not," she explained and wrapped her arms around Able.

"You hit him, alright," Mitchel assured Michelle. He picked up an old black stove pipe lying discarded next to the wood stove and pointed at a few drops of fresh blood next to it. "Unless anyone in this room is bleeding, I would have to say this blood belongs to the killer."

Michelle ran over to Mitchel. She studied the drops of blood with quick eyes. "He's wounded," she said in relief.

"Flesh and blood," Mitchel told Sam. "The killer isn't invincible."

"Nice shooting," Sam congratulated Michelle and patted her on the back. "My bullets didn't do anything but scare the snake. But now," he said in a reluctant tone, "is the time for us to get out of here. The killer is wounded. We don't—"

"No," Momma Peach interrupted Sam. "Mr. Sam, we can't leave until we catch us a killer. We owe this to Mr. Mitchel. This lodge is a part of him. His wife is still alive within these walls...his memories...his life...his heart. If we desert this lodge, we'll be allowing the killer to murder all of the years Mr. Mitchel spent here with his wife. No, sir and no ma'am, we're not running, Mr. Sam. If we do, Mr. Mitchel will die inside of his heart. I can't allow someone I love to die with a broken heart like that, can I? No, sir and no ma'am."

Sam looked hard at Michel. Mitchel was staring at the stove pipe. "Mitchel?" he asked.

"I'm not leaving my lodge," Mitchel spoke in a low voice. "I would rather die. Sure, I'm scared, but I have never been a coward. My wife and I spent many good years here, Sam. I can't leave her. I won't leave her. You can run if you want."

Michelle walked over to Mitchel. She felt tears sting her eyes. "I'm not leaving, either," she promised Mitchel. "You know, before all this craziness started, Able and I were having such a lovely time here. I'm falling in love with Able and, well," Michelle looked into Mitchel's eyes, "I've been thinking a lot about our future. I don't want to die and dying has been on my mind quite a lot lately."

"Really?" Able asked worriedly.

"Really," Michelle replied in a shaky voice. "I want to get married and have children and paint a nursery and have a baby shower...and being a cop means there's a chance I might die and that means I might lose everything my heart aches for." Michelle looked at Momma Peach. She forced a brave smile to her face. "But no matter my dreams, I've always been a police officer first, right, Momma Peach?"

"That's right, baby," Momma Peach said in a proud voice. "My baby is an officer of the law!"

"And the one thing a cop knows is that when he...or she, in my case...starts trying to be too careful, careful can turn into cowardice, and cowardice can get you killed. There's a killer loose and it's my duty to catch him. And I intend to do just that," Michelle promised Mitchel.

Sam stared up at the dark hole in the ceiling. He didn't want anyone he cared about dying at the hands of a cruel killer. He was desperate to flee the lodge and fetch help. However, he also knew that if he deserted his friends, they would be weaker in the face of a cunning killer, and if he deserted Mitchel, the man's heart would die. Sam knew first-hand what deserting your memories felt like—after all, he had been forced to desert his town. "Not a good night to take a walk in the rain, anyway," he finally said gruffly.

Momma Peach beamed. "I knew you wouldn't leave us, baby. My Mr. Sam is a brave man." Momma Peach walked under the hole in the ceiling and studied the dark space above, which was a mess of rafters and cobwebs. Her mind started to think. She drew in a deep breath of air and then stopped breathing altogether. "Perfume," she whispered.

"What?" Sam asked.

Momma Peach slowly exhaled and then licked her lips. "Perfume," Momma Peach said again. "A woman has been in this room."

Sam smelled the air. All he smelled was the wood stove and old books. "Momma Peach, I don't smell perfume."

"I do," Able said in a quick voice. He sniffed the air. "I've always had the nose of a bloodhound...at first I thought it was you, Michelle." He looked at her with a question in her eyes, but she shook her head, puzzled. "The perfume smells...expensive, too," he mused.

Michelle sniffed the air. She didn't smell the perfume. Mitchel attempted to catch a scent of the perfume but failed. "I can't smell anything."

"Smells like...a mature type of perfume...not a perfume a young girl would wear, no, sir and no ma'am," Momma Peach explained and licked her lips again to capture the scent. "Not young, but not elderly, either."

"So the killer is a woman?" Sam asked.

"A woman didn't strangle Heath Penlin and his hired thug to death," Michelle pointed out.

"Michelle, you could have—"

"Both men would have put up a fight," Michelle insisted. "I know I'm a skilled fighter, Sam, but I'm not as strong as a man. My speed and the power of years of training are what benefit me in a fight. Heath Penlin's body didn't show any signs of a struggle, and neither did his criminal friend. Whoever strangled them to death is very strong and knows how exactly to attack and disable a victim with lightning speed."

Momma Peach thought back to a certain pool hall where she and Michelle had spent a memorable afternoon not too long ago. She remembered Michelle tangling with a fat truck driver named Grease. Grease had given Michelle a run for her money. Michelle had won the fight by jumping onto the man's back and applying a fierce chokehold. Even then, it took a couple of minutes for the massive beast of a man to weaken and finally collapse. "Perhaps we have two killers on the loose," Momma Peach ventured in a low voice. "So which killer did you shoot, Michelle?"

Michelle closed her eyes. She saw the person dressed in black climbing up through the hole. She saw herself drop down to one knee and fire off three shots and then she saw...Michelle's eyes flew open. "A hand. I saw a hand reach down in the struggle. I thought the person I shot had fallen over, but that's not it. Someone reached down to yank them up into the ceiling."

"Are you sure?" Sam asked.

Michelle nodded her head. "I think I shot a woman," she said.

Momma Peach looked up at the hole again and then listened to the rain and the wind outside beating at the window with angry hands. "My, my," she said and shook her head.

Duncan Dennerton pulled his mother up through the hole he had cut into the roof. His eyes were dark with fury. "I told you to stay here," he snapped through gritted teeth as his hair was lashed by the rain. "Why didn't you listen to me?"

Charlene Dennerton winced in pain. "My leg..." she gasped as rain splattered down from the dark sky. "I've been shot in my left calf."

Duncan carried his mother to a level area of the roof and sat her down. He ran his hands through his wet black hair, seething. "Why?" he snapped. "I had those people exactly where I wanted them. I was going to kill them off one by one tonight and finish off the old man who owns this place last. Why didn't you stay in position like I ordered you?"

Charlene wrapped her hands around her bleeding calf. She could barely see her son's furious face through the darkness and the rain. Her own face contorted as she was consumed with pain and bitterness. Her features snarled up into an ugly expression. "I knew you would need help."

"I came alone for a reason," Duncan growled. "Mitchel is mine. All mine."

"He killed my husband," Charlene snapped back, "and cost us everything. Our house. Our cars. Our club membership. Our social status. Our life as we knew it. Everything."

Duncan rubbed his hands through his wet hair again and roughly wiped the rain off his brow. "That old man didn't kill dad," he told his mother. "Dad got himself killed in a bad way. But that's not why I'm here. I'm here because of how that old man treated me. No one treats me the way he did and lives. I've planned for this night a long time and now it's time to make that old man suffer."

"You should have stuck by me!" Charlene snapped. "You deserted me instead. Instead of standing by your own mother when she needed you most, you left to join the

Army, didn't you? You deserted your own mother in order to play soldier."

"I needed training," Duncan explained. "I needed time for the old man to relax and forget, too. It was good timing that his old lady died...I found the man alone and broken when I returned..." The corners of his mouth curved into a cold smirk.

"Training? How much training do you need to shoot a man?" Charlene yelled into the rain.

"Oh no," Mitchel grinned, "I wasn't planning on killing Mitchel. I want the man to suffer. My intentions are to kill his guests, frame him for the murders, and watch him rot away in prison. I want the man to suffer."

"You could have told me!" Charlene screamed at Duncan. She forced her mind to calm down amid the howling winds on the rooftop. "When I saw you charged a flight to Alaska on my credit card, I knew where you were going. All I wanted to do, my only son, was help you kill the man who ruined our lives. But you left me behind...yet again." Charlene winced in pain. "When I arrived earlier and saw you lurking around the lodge, I knew there was still time. Still time to help my son get revenge for his family's humiliation."

Duncan felt guilt strike his heart. He was a trained killer, but he had a soft spot in his heart for his mother. After the death of his father, their lives had fallen apart and extreme hardship seemed to spring on them from every corner. Banks wanted money for loans they didn't know about. Family members wanted answers. Bills piled up. Every luxury his mother knew was yanked out from under her feet. "I know we lost our home and the cars and all the good stuff dad gave us. I know it wasn't easy to go live with your sister, but you bounced back and married a rich man. All I care about now is making Mitchel suffer. And I intend to carry out my mission. I'm going to help you back to the truck and you're going to stay there. You're too injured to help now. Are we clear?"

"No," Charlene begged her son, "I want to see Mitchel's face when he realizes the truth. I'll...sit up here on the roof. You go back down into the lodge and finish your business. But don't tell Mitchel before I'm there. Come and get me after you kill off the other guests and get Mitchel tied up."

Duncan hesitated. He raised his face up into the rain and closed his eyes. "Okay," he caved in, "you can remain here on the roof. I'll come and get you after I kill the others." Duncan slowly opened his eyes. "Dad was a cruel man. I hated him for the way he treated us. I'm not doing this for him. I'm doing this for me."

"I know, son," Charlene replied and reached out for Duncan's hand. Duncan pulled away. "I'm sorry for being angry with you. Do you forgive me?"

"Sure," Duncan said and looked over his shoulder. "Sit here. I'll be back for you later."

Duncan walked away and angled his path toward the hole, climbed back down into the roof, and crawled back toward the reading room. He found the reading room empty. "Good," he said to himself and dropped down through the opening in the ceiling, landing on silent feet. "Time to play," he grinned and walked over to the door and eased it open.

Momma Peach was standing out in the hallway, poised and ready.

"Get on out here, you low-down, dirty dog," Momma Peach growled and began swinging her pocketbook at Duncan. "Oh boy am I ever glad I chose to guard this hallway. It's you and me, boy. Get on out here, you filth!"

Duncan couldn't believe his eyes. He searched the long hallway with skilled eyes. Momma Peach was alone. He stepped out into the hallway, reached into the right pocket of his rain coat and pulled out a thin wire, ignoring her swinging purse. He would kill Momma Peach and vanish back into the ceiling before anyone could see him. "Time to die, lady."

Momma Peach stared at Duncan's evil grin and refused to let fear overtake her courage. "Come to Momma Peach, boy, and take your beating." Momma Peach threw her pocketbook at Duncan. Duncan dodged the pocketbook and began stalking toward Momma Peach. Momma Peach crouched down into a silly fighting position and began bouncing around on her short legs like a pit bull. "Come and get some, cause I'm gonna tear you a new one!"

Duncan continued to walk toward Momma Peach. As he did, the doorway to Momma Peach's right flew open. Michelle stepped out into the hallway and positioned herself in front of Momma Peach. Sam, Able and Mitchel followed. Sam aimed his gun straight at Duncan. "We figured you wouldn't give up."

"So it is you," Mitchel said, staring at Duncan.

Duncan took a step back and kicked himself for walking into a trap. The years he had spent training crashed and burned in a flame of failure. He had been certain that his victims would have scattered back downstairs in a pathetic attempt to escape. Why wouldn't they? Surely they must have known the bullets fired up at the ceiling had hit their target. With their attacker wounded, escape was possible. Clearly, he was mistaken. "Yes, it's me," he growled at Mitchel. "Don't act so surprised, old man."

"Why, son?" Mitchel pleaded with Duncan. "I didn't kill your dad. I know we both lost our tempers at each other, but that's no reason to kill innocent people."

"Let's just say I'm not the forgiving type," Duncan spat at Mitchel. "You remember, old man, how you treated me?

You remember pointing your rifle in my face and threatening to kill me, right?"

"Yes," Mitchel said in a sorrowful voice.

"And you remember me telling you to pull the trigger or someday I would return to make you suffer? Oh, yes, you remember. And now the time to suffer has come, old man." Duncan grinned. He focused on Sam. "Shoot me, if you have the guts."

"Don't tempt me," Sam warned Duncan. "Get your hands in the air now!"

Duncan continued to grin. So what if he had walked into a trap? This was just a den of scared, weak cowards, not fighters; or so he thought. "Sure," Duncan said and with one move he threw himself into a forward roll, crashed into Momma Peach, and began wrestling her down to the floor. Momma Peach wasn't going down easy. She began swinging her fists and pounding Duncan in his face.

"Take that, you filthy dog!" Momma Peach hollered. But Duncan was powerful. She felt the man wrap the thin wire in his hands around her throat and pull her back up to her feet at lightning speed. Not one single punch she threw affected the man. Her airpipe could only get the barest breath of air and black spots began to swim in her vision.

"Drop your guns!" Duncan snarled. "All of you, now, or the fat lady dies!"

"Oh no you didn't!" Momma Peach yelled and tried to stomp Duncan with her foot. Duncan pulled the wire tighter against her neck. "Oh yes you did," Momma Peach said and quit fighting.

"Now!" Duncan yelled.

"Do as he says," Michelle ordered. She threw her gun down onto the hallway floor. Sam narrowed his eyes. Rage filled his heart. He threw his gun down and looked at Duncan. "Able, Mitchel, throw your guns down."

Able dropped his gun. Mitchel hesitated and then threw down his gun. "Thanks," Duncan grinned and began pulled Momma Peach back into the reading room. "She dies, you all live...for now. I'll be back for you later, though. The night is still young."

Michelle stepped forward, panicked but holding her cool. "Why don't you stop acting like a coward and fight," she yelled at Duncan. "You and me, pal. No one else. Unless you're useless without that stupid wire," she sneered. "Or are you just scared to fight a woman?"

Duncan froze. He stared at Michelle. The woman was taunting him. Even worse, the woman was disrespecting him.

"He's afraid of a woman," Sam snorted. He knew the only way to save Momma Peach was to get Duncan to fight Michelle and give him enough time to reach his gun.

Duncan growled. He released the garotte wire and shoved Momma Peach forward. Momma Peach went flying into Michelle. Sam tried to catch them, but the force of impact was too much. All he saw was Duncan run forward, kick Able down, shove Mitchel to the side, and snatch up the guns before anyone could react. "Now then," Duncan said and walked back to the reading room door and threw the guns inside the room, "the playing field is even."

"Get that skunk, baby," Momma Peach begged Michelle.

Michelle stood up, helped Momma Peach to her feet, and then focused her attention on Able. Able was helping Mitchel stand up. "Are you okay, honey?"

Able rubbed his chest. "A little sore, but okay."

Momma Peach helped Sam stand up. Sam tried to run at Duncan but Michelle grabbed him. "I can take him, Sam."

Sam looked into Michelle's eyes. "No," he said and pulled away from Michelle, "this is my fight. I know you're not scared, but someday when you and Able get married, I want you to look back on this night and know that...I love you all." Sam walked toward Duncan before Michelle could stop him. "Alright, son, it's time."

"Come and get some, old man."

Sam balled his hands into two fists. "No!" Michelle yelled.

Momma Peach knew Sam couldn't defeat Duncan. But she also knew Sam had to fight. Sam was an old timer, a man of honor, dignity, and courage. Sometimes a man had to stand as a man.

Sam threw a solid punch at Duncan, but Duncan ducked away and punched Sam in the ribs. Sam stumbled backward, caught his breath and charged forward again. Duncan threw a vicious punch at his face. Sam ducked the punch by a hair and managed to get close enough to pound Duncan in his stomach three times. "Not bad, old man," Duncan hissed when he finally escaped and stood up with a red, furious face.

Sam kept his fists in the air. "Shut up and fight."

Duncan charged at Sam, tackled him down to the floor, and began pounding on him. The sight of Sam being hurt sent fury through Momma Peach. "Hold on Mr. Sam, Momma Peach is coming!" Momma Peach charged at Duncan and dived onto his back. Sure, Mr. Sam was a man of dignity, honor, and respect, but she wasn't going to let her baby die at the hands of a filthy alley dog, either. "I'll claw your eyes out!" Momma Peach yelled and wrapped her hands around Duncan's face.

Duncan grabbed Momma Peach's right arm and flung her forward. As Momma Peach rolled forward, she saw Able jump over her body and land a vicious punch upside Duncan's jaw. Duncan went flying backward and crashed down onto the floor. Able jumped on top of him and began landing one punch after another. Momma Peach shot to her feet. "Get him, baby!"

Michelle began to run to Able but Momma Peach grabbed her. "Let your future husband fight this one out, baby."

Michelle wanted to break free from Momma Peach and save Able, but instead, she forced her body to stand still and watch Able fight Duncan. At first, it seemed as if Able was actually winning the fight. Duncan was on his back in a weak defensive mode. Able was throwing one hard punch after the next, pummeling him. But then Duncan wrapped his legs around Able's waist and threw him sideways. Able crashed down onto the hallway floor head first. Duncan rolled on top of him and applied a deadly chokehold. "No!" Michelle screamed and finally broke free from Momma Peach. But before she could reach Able, a single gunshot exploded. Duncan Dennerton stopped choking Able, fell backward, and dropped into an eternal sleep.

Momma Peach looked over at Mitchel. Mitchel lowered the gun he was holding. "I always keep a gun concealed around my ankle. I guess I forgot to tell you folks that," he said in a shaky voice. "Memory ain't as good as it used to be."

Sam crawled to his feet, wiped some blood from his nose, and hurried over to Able. "Are you okay, son?"

Able coughed a few times, looked up into Michelle's beautiful face, and smiled. "I am now."

Momma Peach walked over to Mitchel and hugged him. "My hero," she said and leaned her head down on Mitchel's chest. "Oh, don't I love you."

"You didn't do so bad yourself," Mitchel told Momma Peach and wrapped his arms around her. "We're still missing one killer," he pointed out.

Before anyone could say a word, a horrible shriek filled the hallway. Momma Peach jerked her head up and saw Charlene Dennerton hobble over to her dead son, collapse down onto the floor, and begin weeping. "No...no...what have you done? My poor baby...no..."

Michelle helped Able stand up. With relief, she saw that the wound on the woman's calf was bandaged with a torn scarf, so she would be fine until they could get help. She walked over to Charlene, forced the woman's arms behind her back, and snatched her up. "You have the right to remain silent. Anything you say can and will..."

Momma Peach listened to Michelle read Charlene her Miranda rights. "Mr. Sam, how about some coffee?"

"Sure," Sam said and wiped more blood from his nose.

He looked at Michelle. "We're a family, girl. Never forget that."

Michelle handed Charlene over to Able and hugged Sam. Tears began falling from her eyes. "I love you, too," she whispered in Sam's ear and squeezed him tight. "Thank you, Sam."

"Anytime," Sam smiled. He looked at Able. "Not bad, son, not bad at all."

Able felt proud of himself. He wasn't such a klutz after all. "Next time, I pick where we take a vacation," he said and pushed Charlene down the hallway. Halfway down the hallway he tripped and crashed into her. "Darn shoelaces," he muttered.

"That's our Able," Momma Peach giggled and winked at Michelle. "He'll do just fine."

CHAPTER NINE

Momma Peach watched the teams of law enforcement officers crawling over the North Queen like ants, even though it was raining hard enough to make a whale take cover. "Well, baby," she told Michelle, holding a pink umbrella over her head, "some bad men were arrested today and a bomb was defused. I'd say it's time to go home."

Michelle stared at the North Queen with sadness in her eyes. "Such a beautiful ship, but...so sad," she told Momma Peach. "The ship reminds me of the Titanic for some reason. Doomed. Oh, it looks very pretty and there's a lot of goodies onboard, but that doesn't matter. The heart of that ship is cursed."

"I know, baby."

"Penlin did invest a lot of money into turning that ship

into a strong competitor, but with all its secret cargo spaces and who knows what hidden sabotage, the ship is going to be hauled away and scrapped." Michelle shook her head and focused on the team of crime scene investigators boarding the ship just then with their equipment. She switched the gray umbrella she was holding in her right hand over to her left hand so she could grasp Mama Peach's soft hand in her own. "Well, our work here is finished, Momma Peach. It's time to go home."

"Yes, baby, it is," Momma Peach agreed with a sad heart. She couldn't help but stare at the North Queen with sorrowful eyes. Something about the ship both captivated and scared her at the same time, exactly as it had that fateful day they had first seen it. "I am wondering...why does that ship seem so strange to me?"

"Maybe the size?" Michelle suggested. She looked over her shoulder and spotted a cab idling at the end of the dock. "Our taxi is here, Momma Peach."

Momma Peach nodded her head. She looked at the North Queen one last time and walked to the cab with Michelle. Whatever mysteries the ship held, she could at least rest easy knowing that Heath Penlin and his kind wouldn't be using it for evil schemes any longer.

The cab drove to the airport, where Momma Peach and Michelle boarded their flight back to Georgia. Sam and

Able would remain in Alaska with Mitchel for a couple of weeks. Sam had very quickly made that decision, announcing he would stay to help fix the damage done to the roof and ceilings, and Able had immediately volunteered to help as well. Michelle had not been able to hide her smile of pride in reaction to Able's newfound confidence. Sam and Able knew that more important than manual labor, they needed to offer Mitchel support until he felt comfortable enough being alone. Killing a person took a lot out of a man—a decent man, that is. Mitchel killed Duncan Dennerton because it was a matter of life and death, yet his heart felt heavy with guilt. As much as he didn't want to admit it, he was sure glad Sam and Able decided to hang around the lodge for a couple of weeks.

After the dramatic mountain peaks of the Alaskan wilderness, the lush green gardens and river valleys of Georgia were a welcome view as they took a cab to their little town from the airport. When Momma Peach stepped out of the taxi and soaked in the sight of her bakery, she let out a deep sigh. "Oh, Momma Peach is home," she said in a happy voice.

Michelle stuck her head out of the cab. "I'm heading to the police station, Momma Peach. It's late, but I need to check in. I'll see you tomorrow morning."

"Okay, baby," Momma Peach said. "Mr. Cabbie, drop my luggage off at my house for me, okay?" Momma Peach handed the driver some bills. "Keep the change," she winked.

"Sure thing," the cab driver said in a grateful voice and wrote down Momma Peach's address.

Momma Peach watched the cab pull away with Michelle waving to her from the backseat. It was late and her body felt tired. But the night was clear, cool and peaceful. There wasn't a soul in sight. The town was asleep and she had the main street all to herself.

"Oh me, oh my," she said and walked over to the cast iron table on the porch, tossed her pocketbook onto one chair, and plopped down into the other. "What a time, what a time. If it ain't crazy criminals trying to pull a fast one, it's a crazy killer trying to strangle me to death. Oh me."

Momma Peach lifted her head up and soaked in a night sky glittering with millions of stars. A gentle breeze brushed past her, touched her tired face with loving fingers, and moved on. Momma Peach smiled and thought about the lodge. The lodge sure was nice, and she sure would love to spend time there with Mr. Sam, but Georgia was definitely home. Her bakery was home. The pine trees were home. The little buildings before her on the main street were home; and yes, even the diner with the brick-hard biscuits was home. "Times are changing, though," she murmured to herself. "It won't be long before Michelle and Able say 'I Do' to one another in front of a good preacher man. World's getting to be a crazier place, too. The bad seeds are getting worse and worse by the hour."

Momma Peach heard footsteps. She glanced over her shoulder and saw Old Joe walking up, wearing a clean, pressed white shirt tucked into a nice pair of blue jeans. For once, Old Joe looked honest instead of like a con man on the run. "Hello, Old Joe."

"Don't hello me," Old Joe grumbled. He sat down across from Momma Peach and pointed a finger at her. "Do you know what those two...those...girls of yours did to me?" he demanded. Momma Peach began to answer but Old Joe interrupted her. "They locked me in the cellar, that's what."

Momma Peach chuckled. "They did?"

"They sure did," Old Joe fussed and crossed his arms across his chest. "I've never been so insulted in all my years, Momma Peach. And the worst part is, those...girls of yours...didn't even apologize to me. Oh, they tell Old Joe to sweep the kitchen, take out the trash, wash down shelves...bossy little cats. But they sure don't like showing Old Joe an ounce of compassion."

Momma Peach rolled her eyes. "What did you do to cause my girls to lock you in the cellar, to begin with?"

Old Joe stiffened. "I was conducting some business."

"Oh, give me strength," Momma Peach exclaimed.

"You don't charge enough for your goods, Momma Peach. I simply raised the prices some, that's all."

"'That's all?'" Momma Peach said in a painful voice. "Somebody shoot me and put me out of my misery."

Old Joe bit down on his lower lip. "I...well, I'm a businessman and I decided it wasn't no harm to pocket thirty percent of the profits from the price increase. And hey, that still left you coming out way ahead...until your girls caught me and locked me in the cellar."

"I'll kill you," Momma Peach promised Old Joe calmly. She stood up and grabbed her pocketbook. "Get over here!"

Old Joe hopped to his feet and backed away from Momma Peach. "Now wait a minute, Momma Peach...I was just trying to make us a profit...you know..."

"Profit?" Momma Peach yelled and began advancing toward Old Joe with her pocketbook. "I survive being strangled up on a mountain and I come back to you trying to skim off the top and claim it's a profit?" Old Joe let out a yelp as he stumbled back off the edge of the porch. He recovered his balance and took off running. "Oh, give me strength. If it ain't a crazy criminal, it's Old Joe trying to pull a fast one."

"I'll come by in the morning...you'll feel better then," Old Joe yelled from a distance and vanished down the street.

"I bet you will come by in the morning and eat me out of house and home," Momma Peach said and walked up to the front door of her bakery, unlocked it, and stepped inside. The bakery was dark and smelled of delicious peach bread. Momma Peach shut the front door, looked around the front room, smiled, and began wandering back to the kitchen. As she did, the telephone rang. "Must be Mr. Sam checking in," Momma Peach said and answered the phone. "Momma Peach speaking, how are you, Mr. Sam?"

"You think you've won, but you haven't," a voice spoke in a deathly cold tone.

Momma Peach felt her blood turn cold. "Who am I speaking with?" she asked.

"Your friends will die unless you do as I say," the voice warned Momma Peach. "Bring the cop back to the lodge. We have a game to finish."

"A game?" Momma Peach asked. "If I ain't mistaken, the game ended when Mr. Mitchel killed himself a killer." Momma Peach felt her heart begin racing inside of her chest. Mr. Sam, Able and Mr. Mitchel were in danger.

"Bring the cop back to the lodge," the voice ordered Momma Peach, "or your friends die."

Momma Peach began to speak but stopped when she heard Sam yell: "Don't come back here, Momma Peach!" Then she heard the sickening sound of a fist hitting Sam hard in the face. "I am going to beat you into the grave," she promised the voice. "Yes, sir and yes ma'am."

"Bring the cop back with you. If you try to play any games, your friends will die. The only cop I want to see is your friend, are we clear?" the voice demanded.

"We're clear," Momma Peach said.

"Two days."

Momma Peach hung up the phone. "Oh, give me strength," she said in a shaky voice and hurried to call Michelle. She was told Michelle hadn't reached the police station yet. "Have her call me as soon as she arrives," Momma Peach left a message with the front desk clerk and hurried back into her kitchen. "Think," she told herself. "Who did I just talk with? Who has them captive back in Alaska...a family member of Duncan Dennerton? A brother...uncle...step-brother...best friend...friend of a friend..." Momma Peach racked her brain. "No, Duncan Dennerton acted alone. His mother confessed to flying up to Alaska because she wanted to see poor Mr. Mitchel suffer. Michelle ran a background check, too. Duncan Dennerton was an only child...and Charlene Dennerton never had any children after she remarried, and—" Momma Peach stopped in mid-sentence. "Oh, dear goodness me," she exclaimed. "The trail never ends."

The phone rang out from the bakery. Momma Peach rushed out of her kitchen and snatched up the phone.

"Momma Peach?" Michelle asked, alarmed. "I just received your message," she said, sitting down behind the desk in her office. "What's wrong?"

"Baby, don't get comfy. We have to go back to Alaska. Mr. Sam, Able and Mr. Mitchel are being held prisoner by another killer."

"What?" Michelle exclaimed. She jumped to her feet, Able's sweet face burned into her mind's eye like a brand.

Momma Peach recounted the details of the phone call she received. "I heard Sam warn me not to come back to Alaska, baby. And then I heard the filthy alley dog punch Mr. Sam." She closed her eyes and held back her tears.

"But who?" Michelle begged Momma Peach. Frustration gripped her heart. "I'm sorry, Momma Peach. I know I need to clear my mind, calm down, and think."

Momma Peach bit down on her lower lip. "Baby, call a cab. We're going back to Atlanta and flying up to Alaska."

"Sit tight," Michelle told Momma Peach.

Momma Peach put down the phone. As she did, Old Joe poked his head through the front door. "Momma Peach," he said in a shaky but contrite voice, "I thought maybe...waiting until morning might not be a good idea. Can...we talk?"

Momma Peach stared at Old Joe. Suddenly an idea struck her mind. She ran over to Old Joe and pulled the man into her arms. "Oh, you old sly fox, you're just the weapon Momma Peach needs."

Old Joe began flapping his arms in the air as she tightened her embrace around him. "Okay," he said, confused.

Momma Peach let go of Old Joe and looked into his face. "You're coming to Alaska with me, Old Joe. Michelle will be by shortly. I'll explain on the way. In the meantime, help me pack some bread. We won't have time to stop and eat on the way."

"Alaska?" Old Joe asked and shook his head. "Momma Peach, I ain't no Eskimo."

"You are now, you old poop," Momma Peach told Old Joe and began gathering peach bread off the wooden shelves. Old Joe shrugged his shoulders and began to help. An hour later, he was sitting in the back of a cab with Momma Peach, wondering why in the world she was taking him to Alaska. When he found out, he almost passed out, leaning his forehead against the cool window of the taxi in shock.

Mac Caldwell watched a gray jeep pull up into the gravel parking lot in front of the lodge through the front window of the lobby. He turned his head and focused on the three men sitting tied up and gagged next to the fireplace. "Not a move," he warned and aimed his weapon directly at Mitchel. "Not a word." Sam tried to spit the cloth in his mouth out, but the duct tape wrapped around his mouth was too strong. Able held stock still, trying to control his nerves.

Mac turned his attention back to the jeep, expecting to see Michelle and Momma Peach get out. It was almost dark, which was perfect. He would kill them all tonight and escape into the night with all loose ends tied up. The lodge was so isolated, he doubted anyone would even be able to start tracking his escape for days. Once these loose ends were tied up, he would continue with his medical practice and forget all about his old friend Dr. Dennerton.

The front door to the jeep opened. He saw Michelle step out of the driver's side and...a man crawled out of the passenger's side holding a gun. Mac narrowed his eyes.

"Out!" the man yelled and pointed the gun in his hand at Momma Peach. Momma Peach hurried out of the back seat of the jeep and threw her hands up in the air. "Is this the place? No games!" the man yelled in a furious tone, pressing his gun toward Momma Peach's temple.

"Yes," Momma Peach promised, yelling back. "This is where Heath Penlin was killed."

"I want the money!" the man yelled again and pointed at Michelle. "You, get over here! No games!"

"Okay, stay calm," Michelle told Old Joe and eased over to Momma Peach.

"Where did Penlin hide his millions?" Old Joe demanded. "They're mine now. No games! Do you hear, no games!"

"Heath Penlin didn't arrive at this lodge with any money," Momma Peach insisted.

"You lie!" Old Joe screamed. "Heath Penlin stole the gun money right out from under my nose and traveled up here to this here lodge. I know he brought my money with him!"

"Money?" Mac whispered. He stood very still and watched Old Joe threaten Momma Peach and Michelle.

"I run guns for some dangerous men, woman! And those men want the money they entrusted me with back! So don't talk jive to me. Where is my twenty million?" Old Joe yelled.

"Twenty million dollars?" Mac whispered again. He knew a man by the name of Heath Penlin connected to the Blue Wave cruise line company was murdered, but he wasn't sure why Duncan Dennerton had killed him. Until this moment, he hadn't cared. He assumed Duncan's murderous intentions were purely motivated by a hunger for revenge. But perhaps Duncan had a card up his sleeve.

"I want answers! And don't tell me Duncan didn't talk before he died. Old Joe knows Penlin and Dennerton were working together!"

"So that's it," Mac said to himself, taking the bait hook, line and sinker. He spun away from the window and looked at Mitchel, Sam, and Able. The three men still had to die, but for the time being, they were neutralized. "If you try anything, I'll kill the women, and I'll do it in front of you," he said coldly. Then he ran off toward the kitchen, slipped out of the back door, and began making his way around the lodge, heading for the gravel driveway.

"Where is my money?" Old Joe yelled again. He felt foolish but he had to admit he sure was putting on a fine performance. He only hoped it was good enough to save his own skin, not to mention the poor souls tied up inside.

Mac eased his head around the side of the lodge. He spotted Old Joe aiming the gun in his hand at Momma Peach. The daylight was fading fast. He looked around, surveying the beautiful surrounding trees. He moved away from the lodge and slithered behind a tree in the shadowy underbrush.

Michelle spotted the man duck into the trees and nudged Momma Peach with her elbow. "The rat is taking the bait."

Momma Peach winked at Old Joe. "You're doing fine, you old fox. Now, aim the gun at my head."

Old Joe grinned and then made an angry face. "Where did Penlin and Dennerton hide the money?" Old Joe aimed the gun in his hand at Momma Peach's head, pressing forward again.

"Okay, okay," Momma Peach cried out, pretending to be terrified, though in truth it was not easy having Old Joe hold a gun to her head. "It's true, Mr. Penlin did come up to Alaska with the money. I saw him bury the money down by the lake."

"Do it," Michelle whispered at Old Joe. She feinted to one side as if she was about to take off running. Old Joe hesitated and then aimed at Michelle and fired. The gun erupted. Michelle's body was thrown backward. She collapsed down onto the ground in the gathering darkness.

Momma Peach screamed. "Keep your hands up!" Old Joe yelled at Momma Peach. "No games, woman!"

"No!" Momma Peach cried out. She tried to bend down and check on Michelle. Old Joe grabbed her arm and pushed her forward. "Move" he yelled at her. Momma Peach started walking toward the trail leading down to the lake, sobbing. It was not hard to get into character, imagining her very own baby felled by a bullet and abandoned on the cold ground, even though she knew they were laying a clever trap to catch the rat.

Mac watched her leave Michelle behind. When Old Joe and Momma Peach were far enough away, he left his secure position and began following them, sure that Michelle was dead. He trudged into the approaching night, squinting into the darkness, maintaining a safe distance as he followed the shadowy forms of Old Joe and Momma Peach toward the lake below.

As soon as Mac was out of sight, Michelle climbed to her feet and ran into the lodge. She found Sam, Able and Mitchel tied up. "Oh, you're still alive," she began crying, and pulled off their gags. With shaky hands, she began to untie Able. As soon as Able was free, he jumped to his feet, pulled Michelle into his arms and kissed her.

"We heard a gunshot," said Mitchel worriedly, still tied up on the floor.

"A blank," Michelle explained and kissed Able back. "Hurry, untie Sam. I'll untie Mitchel."

Able hurried and untied Sam. "What's happening? Where's Momma Peach? And why is Old Joe here?" he asked, rubbing his wrist.

"No time to explain. Able, you stay here with Mitchel. Sam, you come with me. We have a killer to catch," Michelle said and kissed Able again.

"I'm coming with you," Able insisted.

"No, honey, not this time," Michelle said in a soft voice. "Three is a crowd. I know you're brave, but this is police business. I intend to capture this killer alive. Please understand. I don't want to risk your life."

Able reached out and took Michelle's hands. "Go," he smiled.

"Hurry," Mitchel urged Michelle.

Michelle nodded her head and hurried out of the front door with Sam at her side. Together, they maneuvered down to the lake on silent feet, quickly covering ground that was covered in a thick carpet of pine needles. When they approached the lake, Michelle spotted Mac crouched down behind a tree. Sam pointed to the dock. "I see Momma Peach and Old Joe," he whispered.

"Okay," Michelle whispered back, "I need a distraction."

"How about an old coyote?" Sam whispered slyly, his eyes crinkling at the corners with a grin.

Michelle bit back a smile. Sometimes she forgot Sam's years battling the desert wilderness. "As soon as you hear my signal, go for it." Michelle vanished into the darkness like a princess warrior.

Sam focused his eyes on Mac and waited. A few minutes later he heard Michelle hoot like a barn owl in the distance, a sound that was almost convincing if you didn't know that barn owls weren't found in Alaska. "Okay," he said, drew in a deep breath of the crisp air, and began a long, mournful coyote howl loud enough to pierce the night and echo against the hills.

Mac instantly jerked, spun around, and searched the darkness. All he could see was dark trees. He knew that was no coyote. As he turned to locate the voice, a fist connected with the side of his face in a vicious sucker punch, dazing him in the darkness. The last thing Mac was conscious of was the sweet smell of a woman's perfume. Then he found himself waking up with his hands handcuffed behind his back, and realized it was Michelle's perfume.

"Clear!" Michelle yelled out. "Momma Peach, Old Joe, you guys can come back from the lake!"

Momma Peach and Old Joe got their legs moving and hurried back up the trail. They found Michelle standing over Mac with Sam at her side. "Who is this idiot anyway?" Old Joe demanded.

"Dr. Mac Caldwell," Sam explained. "Dr. Dennerton's old hunting buddy, as it turns out. Mac Caldwell and his friend, Dr. Richard Burke, murdered Dr. Dennerton and dragged his body out of the safe area."

"But Mitchel said the two men Dr. Dennerton went hunting with were innocent," Michelle said.

"I thought they were," Mitchel spoke. Michelle turned

and saw Mitchel walk down the trail to meet them, with Able at his side. "I guess this old man just wanted to see the good in folk, young lady." Mitchel looked down at Mac, then gestured for them all to step away from the handcuffed man so they could talk. "Caldwell told us all about it while he had us tied up. He and his buddy killed Dr. Dennerton because the man refused to participate in some kind of medical scheme that was supposed to make them millions."

"My, my," Momma Peach said in a disgusted voice.

"That's not all," Able told Momma Peach. "Dr. Caldwell here married Dr. Dennerton's wife Charlene, the woman Michelle shot. Charlene found out about the scheme and had been blackmailing him for money. So that's one more crime that will keep her in jail for many, many years."

"So this rat followed his wife up to Alaska to kill both her and Duncan Dennerton? His own step-son?" Momma Peach asked.

Able nodded sadly. "Caldwell was afraid Duncan knew about the scheme he and his criminal buddy were pulling on the federal Medicaid system. Dr. Caldwell wanted us dead because he was convinced Duncan Dennerton and his mother had spilled the beans to us," Able finished.

"My, my, people sure are evil," Momma Peach said and shook her head. "The bad seeds are getting worse and worse in this old world."

Sam looked at Momma Peach. "Now," he said, "what about the little scheme you just pulled off, huh?" he grinned.

Momma Peach pointed at Old Joe. "Old Joe is to thank," she smiled.

"No, sir and no ma'am, don't think for one second a simple thanks is enough to make this right, Momma Peach," Old Joe grumbled. He looked a little shaky now that the adrenaline had passed, but he tried to pass it off as indignation. "First, your girls lock me in the cellar for a whole day, then you threaten me with bodily harm, then you drag me way up here to Alaska for this foolishness that could have gone wrong a million ways to Sunday. No, sir and no ma'am, Old Joe wants more than a thanks. Perhaps you'll respect Old Joe a bit more now. Give me my due credit. And my profits," he sniffled.

Momma Peach narrowed her eyes, gripped her pocketbook tighter, and looked at Old Joe. "You know what's good for you, you better hush."

"Huh?" Old Joe asked, shocked.

"Actually, I would run," Michelle warned Old Joe.

"Oh," Old Joe said, and got his legs moving and took off toward the lake.

"Give me strength!" Momma Peach yelled out and forced her legs to begin chasing after Old Joe. "Come here, boy.

You want respect from me? I'm gonna beat some respect into that hard head of yours!"

Sam watched Momma Peach disappear into the darkness. "Should I even ask about the foolishness he mentioned? I'm assuming that's what saved us," he said to Michelle with a laugh.

"Don't bother," Michelle said, taking Able's hand, and laughed. "Sam, when it comes to Momma Peach and the way her mind works, it's better not to ask questions."

"Coffee anyone?" Mitchel asked.

"Sure," Michelle giggled, listening to Momma Peach yell at Old Joe to get his back end back to the lodge so she could beat some sense into him. The foul insults in that sweet Georgia accent echoed off the surrounding mountains so she sounded like a giant chasing after him.

"Come on," Sam told Able, "help me get this rat back to the lodge."

Able stood still for a few seconds, regarding the man who had bound and gagged him with pity, before he helped Sam drag Mac back to the lodge. He looked around at the night, soaked in the silence, the wind, the tranquil beauty of the lake, the trees, the lush land, and then he looked into Michelle's beautiful face. "So this is what it feels like to be part of a family," he said.

"I think so," Michelle smiled. "Come on, I could use a cup of coffee."

As they headed up the trail, the echoes of Momma Peach's hollers were finally joined by a mighty splash, and Michelle stifled a giggle as she pictured Old Joe jumping into the lake to swim for safety.

CHAPTER TEN

*M*omma Peach plopped her pocketbook down onto the counter of her bakery and pointed at Old Joe. He stood where he had just put down their luggage. He was a chastened man, after he had been dragged out of the lake by the scruff of his neck. In the end, even Momma Peach wouldn't let him drown. "I am cranky and sleepy, so don't start in on me. Just go into the kitchen and pour me a glass of milk."

"Sure, sure," Old Joe said, holding out his hands palm-first as if he was trying to calm a mama grizzly bear, and backed away into the kitchen.

Momma Peach rolled her eyes and calmed her mind. "Maybe this time I can rest," she said.

"Maybe," Sam yawned and stretched his arms. "I sure

could use a good night's sleep, Momma Peach. My mind is exhausted."

"Well, baby, at least some very bad people are behind bars. Dr. Caldwell confessed to helping his friend kill poor Dr. Dennerton, and Heath Penlin's criminal friends are behind bars for a while."

Sam leaned against the front counter. "From what Dr. Caldwell confessed, Dr. Dennerton wasn't as innocent as he seemed. Sure, the man didn't agree at first to pull the wool over the government's eyes, but it wasn't long before he was writing out a lot of illegal prescriptions and pocketing a nice percentage in return."

"Oh, I know, baby," Momma Peach told Sam. "It's just...well, when a man is murdered, ganged up on by two of his friends like that, and then abandoned out there in the cold snowy wilderness...somehow he seems square with the house."

Sam nodded his head. "Yeah, that's true," he agreed. "Speaking of houses, I better get to my house and see if the electricity is still on."

Momma Peach chuckled. "It has been quite a trip, hasn't it?"

Sam nodded, then turned his head when he heard her sigh sadly. "Momma Peach?" he asked.

Momma Peach gave a sad smile and walked over to the front display window. She looked out into an early Georgia morning blossoming to life. She saw old friends arriving at their stores and familiar faces walking down the sidewalk. "Mr. Sam, you're still going to buy Mr. Mitchel's lodge?"

"Yes, Momma Peach," Sam said. He walked over to Momma Peach and put his hands down onto her shoulders. "I really want to own that lodge someday. But you heard Mitchel. He won't be ready to sell his lodge for a few more years."

Momma Peach patted Sam's hand. "I worry I might lose you altogether if you buy the lodge."

Sam turned Momma Peach around and looked deep into her eyes. "You're never going to lose me, lady," he promised and kissed Momma Peach on the nose. "Momma Peach, we're a family."

Momma Peach felt a tear fall from her eye. She hugged Sam. "Oh, I feel the same way. Now—" Momma Peach stopped talking when she heard the phone sitting on the front counter ring. "I better answer that call. But I swear, upon a stack of my secret recipes, if there is another killer on the line, he is going to have to wait until tomorrow for me to fly back to Alaska. Give me strength! After all, I still have a bakery to run."

Despite her fatigue, Momma Peach bustled over to the

front counter and picked up the phone. "Momma Peach speaking."

"Who is this?" Aunt Rachel asked. "Louise, is that you?"

Momma Peach let out a painful whimper and looked at Sam with terrified eyes. "It's her," she said and began banging the phone against her head. Somehow, she would have preferred a killer on the line at that moment.

"Louise?" Aunt Rachel asked. "Louise, speak to me!"

"This is not Louise!" Momma Peach cried into the phone. "Aunt Rachel, this is your niece...Caroline Johnson!"

Aunt Rachel cackled. "I don't live in Carolina," she told Momma Peach, pretending to sound feeble-minded. "Louise, are you taking your medicine? Is Bob giving you your pill?"

"Who is Bob?" Momma Peach cried. "Aunt Rachel, this is Caroline Johnson and—"

"I've got gas," Aunt Rachel interrupted. "Charlie made beans again last night. He knows beans give me gas, too."

"So don't eat beans," Momma Peach hollered into the phone. "And who is Charlie...oh, give me strength!"

Sam began easing toward the front door. He had heard about Aunt Rachel and didn't want any part of the conversation. "Oh, no you don't," Momma Peach said.

She ran over, grabbed Sam, pulled him back to the front counter and shoved the phone into his hand. "Aunt Rachel, say hello to my friend Sam."

Sam flinched. He raised the phone up to his ear. "Uh...hello, Aunt Rachel."

"Charlie, is that you? What are you doing at Bob's house? You should be home cooking my beans," Aunt Rachel fussed at Sam.

Momma Peach winked at Sam. "Family suffers together," she said and ran into the kitchen. She found Old Joe sitting on her baking table, drinking a glass of cold milk. When Old Joe saw Momma Peach he knew he was in trouble and hopped down instantly. "You dare sit on my baking table like you're back home on the couch, drinking my milk, without taking me a glass first?" Momma Peach asked Old Joe. She walked over the back door and picked up a broom.

"Now wait a minute, Momma Peach, please," Old Joe begged.

Momma Peach shook her head. "I am going to sweep you right out of the back door!"

Old Joe backed up to the kitchen sink and prepared for the worst. But before Momma Peach could reach him, Michelle walked into the kitchen. She looked at Momma Peach, the broom, and then over at Old Joe who had his hands held out in front of his face. "Should I come back?" she asked.

"No, baby," Momma Peach grinned, "you can stay and watch the performance."

"Speaking of performances," Michelle told Momma Peach in a voice that caused Momma Peach's ears to perk up, "there's a new case."

"Oh, give me strength," Momma Peach said and lowered the broom in her hands. "Scat!" she yelled at Old Joe. Old Joe ran out of the kitchen, found Sam banging the phone against his head, decided everyone was nuts and hurried out into the fresh, beautiful morning for some air.

Michelle walked over to the kitchen sink and turned on the cold water. "The circus is in town," she said and splashed water onto her face. "A man by the name of Lance Potter was found dead in his trailer."

"Please tell me an elephant sat on the poor soul," Momma Peach begged.

"No, Momma Peach," Michelle said. She took a dry dish towel and wiped at her sleepy face. "Lance Potter is part of the clown group traveling with the Fantastic Circus. It was a murder. Seems like we're about to investigate a clown mystery, Momma Peach."

Momma Peach poured herself a glass of milk, listened to Sam beg Aunt Rachel to stop talking about her bowel movements, and shook her head. "A dead clown in my hometown. Let's just hope the clown wasn't killed with a funny bone," Momma Peach told Michelle and drank her milk, thinking about how crazy the world was.

Michelle leaned back against the kitchen sink and yawned. Sure, she was exhausted, but life was good. She and Able and everyone she loved had returned safely from Alaska. Even though she was in love and wanted nothing more than to curl up with her boyfriend, she was still a cop who had a job to do...just as long as Momma Peach was at her side.

"Well, as Isaiah says in the Good Book," Momma Peach said, smiling at Michelle, "the wicked have no peace, sayeth the Lord."

Miles away, striped circus tents clustered in an open field in the quiet morning air. A hideous face stalked silently into the main circus tent and searched for his next victim with a wicked smile.

ABOUT THE AUTHOR

Wendy Meadows is an emerging author of cozy mysteries. She lives in "The Granite State" with her husband, two sons, two cats and lovable Labradoodle.

When she isn't working on her stories she likes to tend to her flowers, relax with her pets and play video games with her family.

Get in Touch with Wendy
www.wendymeadows.com

a   amazon.com/author/wendymeadows

g   goodreads.com/wendymeadows

BB   bookbub.com/authors/wendy-meadows

f   facebook.com/AuthorWendyMeadows

🐦   twitter.com/wmeadowscozy

70492047R00126

Made in the USA
San Bernardino, CA
02 March 2018